The Ne

About the Book

G000088729

The New Observ pensable annual aeroplanes and h of established ai nual edition, emb... variable-geometry aeroplanes and ... twenty-three countries. Its scope ranges from such general aviation newcomers as the Beechcraft Starship and Gates-Piaggio Avanti, through the latest airliners, such as the BAe ATP and Fokker 100, to such technology demonstrators for next-generation combat aircraft as the BAe EAP and Dassault-Breguet Rafale, and new warplanes as represented by the IAI Lavi fighter. The latest available information is provided on recently-introduced Soviet military aircraft, including the MiG-29 *Fulcrum* and Su-27 *Flanker*, the principal military and civil aeroplanes now being produced in China, and new variants of many established types,. All data have been checked and revised as necessary, and more than half of the three-view silhouettes are new or have been revised.

About the Author

William Green, compiler of *The New Observer's Book of Aircraft* for 35 years, is internationally known for many works of aviation reference. William Green entered aviation journalism during the early years of World War II, subsequently serving with the RAF and resuming aviation writing in 1947. He is currently managing editor of one of the largest-circulation European-based aviation journals, *AIR International*, and co-editor of *AIR Enthusiast* and the *RAF Yearbook*.

As well as the paperback *New Observer's* guides, there are hardback *Observer's* too, covering a wide range of topics.

NATURAL HISTORY   Birds   Bird's Eggs   Wild Animals   Farm Animals   Sea Fishes   Butterflies   Larger Moths   Caterpillars   Sea and Seashore   Cats   Trees   Grasses   Cacti   Gardens   Roses   House Plants   Vegetables   Geology   Fossils

SPORT AND LEISURE   Golf   Tennis   Sea Fishing   Music   Folk Song   Jazz   Big Bands   Sewing   Furniture   Architecture   Churches

COLLECTING   Awards and Medals   Glass   Pottery and Porcelain   Silver   Victoriana   Firearms   Kitchen Antiques

TRANSPORT   Small Craft   Canals   Vintage Cars   Classic Cars   Manned Spaceflight   Unmanned Spaceflight

TRAVEL AND HISTORY   London   Devon and Cornwall   Cotswolds   World Atlas   European Costume   Ancient Britain   Heraldry

The New Observer's Book of
Aircraft

Compiled by
William Green

with silhouettes by
Dennis Punnett

Describing 142 aircraft
with 247 illustrations

1986 edition

Frederick Warne

FREDERICK WARNE

Penguin Books Ltd, Harmondsworth, Middlesex, England
Viking Penguin Inc., 40 West 23rd Street, New York, New York 10010, U.S.A.
Penguin Books Australia Ltd, Ringwood, Victoria, Australia
Penguin Books Canada Limited, 2801 John Street, Markham, Ontario, Canada L3R 1B
Penguin Books (N.Z.) Ltd, 182–190 Wairau Road, Auckland 10, New Zealand

Thirty-fifth edition 1986

ISBN 0 7232 3362 4

Printed in Great Britain by Butler & Tanner Ltd, Frome and London

INTRODUCTION TO THE 1986 EDITION

NINETEEN HUNDRED AND EIGHTY-SIX will, it is anticipated, be something of a vintage year in combat aircraft development annals, for it will witness the début in flight test or service of several noteworthy new military aircraft which are to be found in this, the thirty-fifth annual edition of *The New Observer's Book of Aircraft*. Of these, a foretaste of the likely configuration of fighter aircraft entering service in the 'nineties is provided by two advanced fighter technology demonstration aircraft embodying a number of innovatory features, British Aerospace's EAP and Dassault-Breguet's Rafale. In Israel, the flight development programme of the Lavi fighter is expected to commence and preliminary details of this new aircraft are included in the following pages, together with the latest details of two Soviet fighters, the MiG-29 *Fulcrum* and the Su-27 *Flanker*, which should be deployed during the course of the year.

On the civil side and scarcely less innovatory than these military types are the radical Beechcraft Starship and Gates-Piaggio Avanti light corporate transports, which, together with the dramatically redesigned and equally advanced Avtek 400, will emerge this year. The most recent information relating to these aircraft, accompanied by new drawings, appears in this edition, together with other civil debutantes, such as the British Aerospace ATP and Fokker 100 regional airliners, derivatives of the classic BAe 748 and F28, which, dating back a quarter-century and two decades respectively, have appeared in many earlier editions of this publication.

As in the past, *The New Observer's Book of Aircraft* is devoted primarily to the most recent aircraft types—including those expected to appear during the year of the volume's currency—and the latest variants of established types rather than those aircraft most commonly seen in the world's skies. All data given for aircraft reappearing from previous editions are updated in the light of information provided by their manufacturers or gleaned from intelligence sources. The accompanying general arrangement silhouettes have been carefully checked for any modifications or changes that may be applied to the aircraft concerned. In this edition, more than half of the drawings are either new or have been revised since they last appeared.

WILLIAM GREEN

AERITALIA-AERMACCHI-EMBRAER AMX

Countries of Origin: Italy and Brazil.
Type: Single-seat battlefield support and light attack aircraft.
Power Plant: One 11,030 lb st (5 000 kgp) Rolls-Royce Spey Mk 807 Turbofan.
Performance: Max speed, 720 mph (1 160 km/hr) or Mach = 0·95 at 1,000 ft (305 m); average cruise, 590 mph (950 km/h) or Mach = 0·77 at 2,000 ft (610 m); combat radius (with 3,000 lb/1 360 kg ordnance, two 110 Imp gal/500 l drop tanks, 10 min reserves and allowance for 5 min combat), 230 mls (370 km) LO-LO-LO, 323 mls (520 km) HI-LO-LO-HI; ferry range (two 220 Imp gal/1 000 l external tanks), 1,840 mls (2 965 km).
Weights: Operational empty, 14,770 lb (6 700 kg); typical mission, 23,700 lb (10 750 kg); max take-off, 26,896 lb (12 200 kg).
Armament: (Italian) One 20-mm M61A1 rotary cannon or (Brazilian) two 30 mm DEFA 553 cannon, two AIM-9L or similar AAMs at wingtips and max external load of 8,377 lb (3 800 kg) distributed between five hardpoints.
Status: First of six prototypes (A01) flown 15 May 1984, with second (A02) and third (A03) following 19 November 1984 and 28 January 1985. A replacement for the first prototype which was lost on its fifth flight was flown on 24 May 1985 (A11), and the first Brazilian-assembled prototype (A04) was flown on 16 October 1985. Current planning calls for 187 and 79 production aircraft for the Italian and Brazilian air forces respectively.
Notes: The AMX is being developed by Aeritalia (47·1%) and Aermacchi (23·2%) in Italy, and Embraer (29·7%) in Brazil, without component production duplication. A two-seat version was under development at the beginning of 1986.

AERITALIA-AERMACCHI-EMBRAER AMX

Dimensions: Span 29 ft 1½ in (8,87 m); Length, 44 ft 6½ in (13,57 m); height, 15 ft 0¼ in (4,58 m); wing area, 226·05 sq ft (21,00 m²).

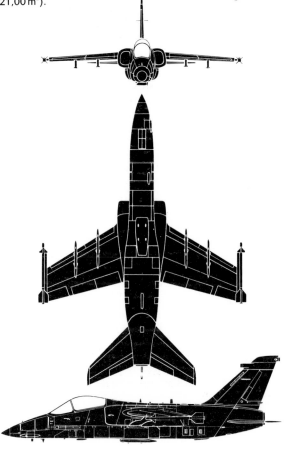

AERITALIA-PARTENAVIA AP68TP-600 VIATOR

Country of Origin: Italy.
Type: Light utility transport.
Power Plant: Two 328 shp Allison 250-B17C turboprops.
Performance: (MP Viator) Max cruising speed, 248 mph (398 km/h) at 12,000 ft (3 660 m); range cruise, 196 mph (315 km/h at 5,000 ft (1 525 m); max range (standard fuel), 1,030 mls (1 658 km) at 196 mph (315 km/h), (with auxiliary fuel), 1,459 mls (2 348 km), (at max cruise), 817 mls (1 316 km), (with auxiliary fuel), 1,161 mls (1 868 km); initial climb, 1,850 ft/min (9,4 m/sec); service ceiling, 25,000 ft (7 625 m).
Weights: (MP Viator) Empty, 3,748 lb (1 780 kg); max take-off, 6,283 lb (2 850 kg).
Accommodation: Pilot and co-pilot/passenger in cockpit with four rows of paired individual seats in main cabin, or (MP Viator) pilot and three systems operators.
Status: Derived from the Spartacus RG (see 1985 edition) which was first flown in July 1984, the Viator (originally Spartacus 10RG) was first flown on 29 March 1985, production deliveries being scheduled to commence during 1986.
Notes: The Viator (Wayfarer) is a progressive development of the P68 first flown in 1970, and an extrapolation of the fixed-gear AP68TP-300 Spartacus (see 1984 edition) via the Spartacus RG (see 1985 edition). The Viator introduces a 25·6-in (65-cm) fuselage stretch and is proposed in maritime surveillance (MP Viator) form with 360-deg search and SLAR radar.

AERITALIA-PARTENAVIA AP68TP-600 VIATOR

Dimensions: Span, 39 ft 4½ in (12,00 m); length, 35 ft 7¼ in (11,55 m); height, 11 ft 11¼ in (3,64 m); wing area, 200·23 sq ft (18,60 m²).

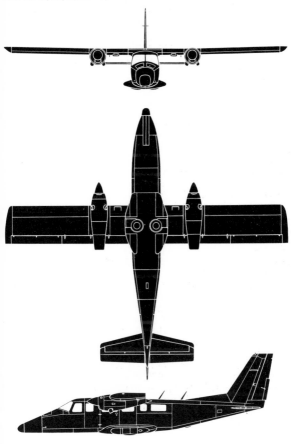

AERMACCHI MB-339

Country of Origin: Italy.

Type: Tandem two-seat basic/advanced trainer and light attack aircraft.

Power Plant: One (MB-339A) 4,000 lb st (1 814 kgp) Fiat-built Rolls-Royce Viper 632-43 or (MB-339B and -339C) 4,450 lb st (2 018 kgp) Viper 680-43 turbojet.

Performance: (MB-339A) Max speed, 558 mph (898 km/h) or Mach=0·73 at sea level, 508 mph (817 km/h) or Mach=0.75 at 30,000 ft (9 145 m); max initial climb, 6,195 ft/min (33,5 m/sec); time to 30,000 ft (9 145 m), 7·1 min; ferry range, 1,311 mls (2 110 km).

Weights: Empty equipped, 6,889 lb (3 125 kg); loaded (clean), 9,700 lb (4 400 kg); max take-off, 12,996 lb (5 895 kg).

Armament: Up to 4,000 lb (1 815 kg) of ordnance distributed between six wing hardpoints.

Status: First of two (MB-339A) prototypes flown 12 August 1976, and first of 100 for Italian Air Force handed over on 8 August 1979. Twelve MB-339As have been exported to each of Dubai and Nigeria, 16 to Peru and 12 to Malaysia.

Notes: The MB-339B (illustrated above) is essentially similar to the MB-339A apart from the uprated Viper engine, and the similarly-powered MB-339C differs in having new mission avionics, a head-up display and improved navigation equipment. The MB-339C, the first prototype of which was scheduled to enter test at the end of 1985, can carry Sistel Marte anti-shipping missiles, as well as the Hughes Maverick air-to-surface and Sidewinder air-to-air missiles, and will be available for delivery in 1987. The MB-339K (see 1981 edition) is a dedicated single-seat light close air support model which may be fitted with similar avionics to those of the MB-339C.

AERMACCHI MB-339

Dimensions: Span 35 ft 7 in (10,86 m); length, 36 ft 0 in (10,97 m); height, 13 ft 1 in (3,99 m); wing area, 207·74 sq ft (19,30 m²).

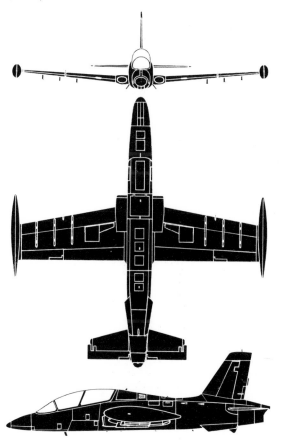

AEROSPATIALE TB 30 EPSILON

Country of Origin: France.

Type: Tandem two-seat primary/basic trainer.

Power Plant: One 300 hp Avco Lycoming AEIO-540-L1B5-D six-cylinder horizontally-opposed engine.

Performance: (At 3,086 lb/1 400 kg) Max speed, 236 mph (380 km/h) at sea level; max cruise (75% power), 222 mph (358 km/h) at 6,000 ft (1 830 m); max initial climb, 1,850 ft/min (9,4 m/sec); service ceiling, 23,000 ft (7 010 m); endurance (60% power), 3·75 hrs.

Weights: Empty equipped, 2,922 lb (917 kg); loaded (aerobatic), 2,756 lb (1 250 kg); max take-off, 3,086 lb (1 400 kg).

Armament: (Export) Four underwing hardpoints stressed to carry 352 lb (160 kg) inboard and 176 lb (80 kg) outboard. Alternative loads include two twin 7,62-mm machine gun pods, four six-rocket (68-mm) pods, or two 264·5-lb (120-kg) bombs.

Status: Two prototypes flown on 22 December 1979 and 12 July 1980 respectively, and first production Epsilon flown on 29 June 1983. The Epsilon entered *Armée de l'Air* service late 1984, and the service has a total requirement for 150 aircraft. Three of the armed export version have been ordered by Togo. Production rate was running at three monthly at the beginning of 1986.

Notes: The first prototype Epsilon has been fitted with a 300 shp Turboméca TP 319 turboprop with which it was first flown on 9 November 1985. This is to serve primarily as a test-bed for the TP 319, but Aérospatiale was considering development of a production version for the export market at the beginning of 1986. The Turbo Epsilon is not expected to differ from the basic Epsilon in any major respect aft of the firewall.

AEROSPATIALE TB 30 EPSILON

Dimensions: Span, 25 ft 11½ in (7,92 m); length, 24 ft 10½ in (7,59 m); height, 8 ft 8¾ in (2,66 m); wing area, 103·34 sq ft (9,60 m²).

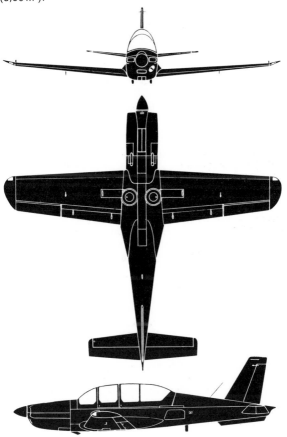

AEROSPATIALE-AERITALIA ATR 42

Countries of Origin: France and Italy.
Type: Regional commercial transport.
Power Plant: Two 1,800 shp Pratt & Whitney Canada PW120 turboprops.
Performance: (ATR 42-300) Max cruising speed, 307 mph (495 km/h) at 20,000 ft (6 095 m); econ cruise, 292 mph (470 km/h) at 25,000 ft (7 620 m); max initial climb, 1,860 ft/min (9,40 m/sec); range (with 46 passengers and reserves), 978 mls (1 575 km) at econ cruise, (with max fuel), 2,647 mls (4 260 km).
Weights: (ATR 42-300) Operational empty, 21,986 lb (9 973 kg); max take-off, 35,605 lb (16 150 kg).
Accommodation: Flight crew of two with four-abreast seating for 42 passengers with optional arrangement for 50 passengers at reduced pitch.
Status: First of three prototypes flown on 16 August 1984, with certification achieved on 24 September 1985. The ATR 42 was scheduled to enter service in December 1985 with Air Littoral of France and Cimber Air of Denmark, and the first US delivery (to Command Airways) was expected to take place in January 1986. By the beginning of December 1985, orders had been placed for 54 aircraft and 39 options had been taken, including eight for the ATR 72.
Notes: Developed and manufactured on a 50-50 basis by Aérospatiale of France and Aeritalia of Italy, the ATR (*Avion de Transport Régional*) 42 is available in -200 and -300 versions, the former having a gross weight of 34,725 lb (15 750 kg), and, from 1988, in stretched ATR 72 form, the last-mentioned having 2,000 shp PW124 engines and accommodation for 60–70 passengers.

14

AEROSPATIALE-AERITALIA ATR 42

Dimensions: Span, 80 ft 7½ in (24,57 m); length, 74 ft 5½ in (22,67 m); height, 24 ft 10¾ in (7,59 m); wing area 586·65 sq ft (54,50 m²).

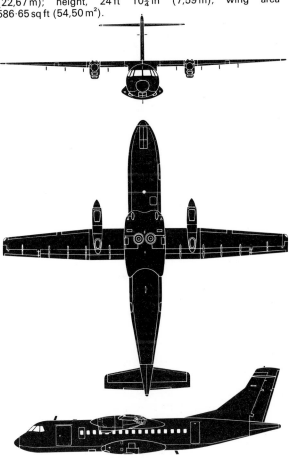

AIDC AT-3 TSE TCHAN

Country of Origin: Taiwan.

Type: Tandem two-seat basic/advanced trainer.

Power Plant: Two 3,500 lb st (1 588 kgp) Garrett TPE731-2-2L turbofans.

Performance: Max speed, 560 mph (900 km/h) at 36,000 ft or Mach=0·85, 558 mph (898 km/h) at sea level or Mach=0·73; max initial climb, 8,000 ft/min (40,64 m/sec); service ceiling, 48,000 ft (14 630 m); max endurance (internal fuel), 3·2 hrs.

Weights: Empty equipped, 8,500 lb (3 855 kg); normal loaded (training mission), 11,500 lb (7 485 kg); max take-off, 16,500 lb (7 485 kg).

Armament: (Weapons training and light strike) Bay beneath rear cockpit for bombs or semi-recessed gun packs, various ordnance loads up to 4,000 lb (1 815 kg) distributed between one fuselage and four wing hardpoints, and provision for two AIM-9J Sidewinder AAMs on wingtip stations.

Status: Two (XAT-3) prototypes flown on 16 September 1980 and 30 October 1981 respectively, and first production aircraft flown on 6 February 1984 against initial contract for 50 plus aircraft.

Notes: The AT-3 Tse Tchan (Self-sufficiency) is a combat-capable aircraft designed by the Aerospace Industry Development Centre (AIDC), a subsidiary of the Chung Shan Institute of Science and Technology. Designed specifically to replace the Lockheed T-33A advanced trainer in the inventory of the Nationalist Chinese Air Force, the Tse Tchan has a secondary light strike role, and follow-on production batches are expected to be produced specifically for this task with upgraded avionics and enhanced weapons capability.

AIDC AT-3 TSE TCHAN

Dimensions: Span, 34 ft 4 in (10,46 m); length (including probe), 42 ft 4 in (12,90 m); height, 14 ft 3½ in (4,36 m); wing area, 236·06 sq ft (21,93 m²).

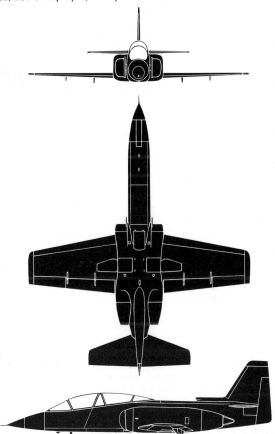

AIRBUS A300-600

Country of Origin: International consortium.

Type: Medium-haul commercial airliner.

Power Plant: Two 56,000 lb st (25 400 kgp) Pratt & Whitney JT9D-7R4H1 or General Electric CF6-80C2 turbofans.

Performance: Max cruise speed, 554 mph (891 km/h) at 31,000 ft (9 450 m); econ cruise, 536 mph (862 km/h) at 33,000 ft (10 060 m); range cruise, 518 mph (833 km/h) at 35,000 ft (10 670 m); range (max payload), 3,430 mls (5 200 km) at econ cruise, (max fuel with 52,900-lb/23 995-kg payload), 5,320 mls (8 560 km).

Weights: Operational empty, 193,410 lb (87 728 kg); max take-off, 363,760 lb (165,000 kg).

Accommodation: Flight crew of three and maximum seating for 344 passengers, a typical arrangement being for 267 passengers in a mixed-class layout.

Status: First JT9D-powered A300-600 flown on 8 July 1983, with first customer delivery (to Saudia) following in May, and first CF6-powered –600 flown on 20 March 1985. Total of 272 A300s (all versions) ordered by December 1985 when 256 delivered. Production rate (including A310) three per month at beginning of 1986.

Notes: The A300 is manufactured by a consortium of Aérospatiale (France), British Aerospace (UK), Deutsche Airbus (Federal Germany) and CASA (Spain). The latest version, the A300-600, replaces the A300B4-200 (see 1983 edition) from which it differs primarily in having the new, re-profiled rear fuselage of the A310 with an extension of the parallel portion of the fuselage offering an 18-seat increase in passenger capacity, and later-generation engines as offered with the A310. The first CF6-80C2-powered –600 was delivered to the launch customer, Thai International, during September of 1985, and the extended-range A300-600ER will be introduced in 1986.

AIRBUS A300-600

Dimensions: Span, 147 ft 1¼ in (44,84 m); length, 177 ft 5 in (54,08 m); height, 54 ft 3 in (16,53 m); wing area, 2,799 sq ft (260,00 m²).

AIRBUS A310-300

Country of Origin: International consortium.
Type: Medium-range commercial transport.
Power Plant: Two 50,000 lb st (22 680 kg) Pratt & Whitney JT9D-7R4E or General Electric CF6-80C2-A2 turbofans.
Performance: Max cruising speed, 561 mph (903 km/h) at 35,000 ft (10 670 m); long-range cruise, 534 mph (860 km/h) at 37,000 ft (11 280 m); range (with max payload), 4,318 mls (6 950 km) at econ cruise, (max fuel), 6,034 mls (9 710 km) at long-range cruise.
Weights: Operational empty, 169,840 lb (77 040 kg); max take-off, 330,688 lb (150,000 kg).
Accommodation: Flight crew of two or three with 280 passengers with single-class seating eight abreast, or 218 passengers in a typical mixed-class (first and economy) layout.
Status: The first A310-300 was flown on 8 July 1985, and was scheduled for certification and delivery to launch customer (Swissair) in December 1985, with CF6-powered version being scheduled for certification in February 1986, with service entry (by Air India) in the following June. First A310 flown on 3 April 1982, and 117 ordered by beginning of December 1985, with 72 delivered. Production rate (including A300—see pages 18-19) three monthly.
Notes: The A310-300 differs from earlier A310 models in having an additional fuel tank in the tailplane, a carbonfibre-reinforced plastic fin, wingtip fences and a revised cockpit. By comparison with the earlier A300B, the A310 has a new, higher aspect ratio wing, a shorter fuselage, a new tailplane and a new undercarriage, but it retains a high degree of commonality with the preceding and larger aircraft. Empty weight of -300 is very similar to -200 despite higher MTOW.

AIRBUS A310-300

Dimensions: Span, 144 ft 0 in (43,90 m); length, 153 ft 1 in (46,66 m); height, 51 ft 10 in (15,81 m); wing area, 2,357·3 sq ft (219,00 m²).

ANTONOV AN-28 (CASH)

Country of Origin: Poland (USSR licence).
Type: Light STOL utility transport.
Power Plant: Two 960 shp PZL-Rzészow-built Glushenkov PZL-10S (TVD-10B) turboprops.
Performance: Max cruising speed, 217 mph (350 km/h) at 9,850 ft (3 000 m); econ cruise, 208 mph (335 km/h) at 9,850 ft (3 000 m); max initial climb, 1,575 ft/min (8,0 m/sec); range (max payload), 348 mls (560 km), (max fuel), 848 mls (1 365 km).
Weights: Empty equipped, 8,267 lb (3 750 kg); max take-off, 14,330 lb (6 500 kg).
Accommodation: Flight crew of two and basic arrangement (light regional transport role) for 15 passengers three abreast with offset aisle, or up to 20 seats in high-density configuration. An aeromedical version can accommodate six casualty stretchers, five seated casualties and a medical attendant.
Status: Initial prototype flown (as An-14M) in September 1969, with production prototype following early in 1974. Further pre-series aircraft produced in Soviet Union before, in 1978, entire manufacturing programme transferred to Poland where five were produced in 1984, 30 in 1985, with production tempo building up at the beginning of 1986 to a planned 200 aircraft annually.
Notes: The An-28 is manufactured by PZL-Mielec under the CMEA co-operative programme and is intended primarily as a successor to the An-2 biplane in many of its roles. Current planning calls for the supply of 1,200 An-28s to the Soviet Union by 1990, the utility transport having successfully passed Aeroflot service trials late 1985, with regular service entry planned for 1986.

ANTONOV AN-28 (CASH)

Dimensions: Span, 72 ft 5¼ in (22,08 m); length, 42 ft 10¼ in (12,98 m); height, 14 ft 9⅛ in (4,50 m); wing area, 428·4 sq ft (39,80 m²).

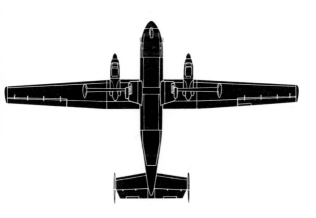

ANTONOV AN-32 (CLINE)

Country of origin: USSR.

Type: Military tactical transport.

Power Plant: Two 4,195 ehp Ivchenko AI-20M or 5,180 ehp AI-20DM turboprops.

Performance: (AI-20DM engines) Normal continuous cruise, 329 mph (530 km/h) at 26,250 ft (8 000 m); service ceiling, 29,525 ft (9 000 m); range with 45 min reserves (max fuel), 1,367 mls (2 200 km), (max payload), 487 mls (800 km).

Weights: (AI-20DM engines) Max take-off, 59,525 lb (27 000 kg).

Accommodation: Flight crew of five and 39 troops on tip-up seats along fuselage sides, 30 fully-equipped paratroops or 24 casualty stretchers and one medical attendant. A max of 14,770 lb (6 700 kg) of freight may be carried.

Status: Based on the An-26 (Curl), the An-32 was first flown in prototype form late 1976, production of a more powerful version (AI-20DM engines) developed specifically to meet an Indian requirement being initiated in 1982. Deliveries against an Indian order for 95 aircraft commenced in July 1984.

Notes: The AI-20DM-powered An-32 is intended specifically for operation under high temperature conditions or from high-altitude airfields. It features triple-slotted wing trailing-edge flaps and automatic leading-edge slats, and has low-pressure tyres to permit operation from unpaved strips. Named Sutlej (after the Punjabi river) in Indian Air Force service, the An-32 is reported to have been ordered by Tanzania, but the only major customer announced by the beginning of 1986 was India. The An-32 can accommodate various small wheeled or tracked vehicles which may be airdropped via a rear loading hatch and forward-sliding ramp-door.

ANTONOV AN-32 (CLINE)

Dimensions: Span, 95 ft 9½ in (29,20 m); length, 77 ft 8¼ in (23,68 m); height, 28 ft 8½ in (8,75 m); wing area, 807·1 sq ft (74,98 m²).

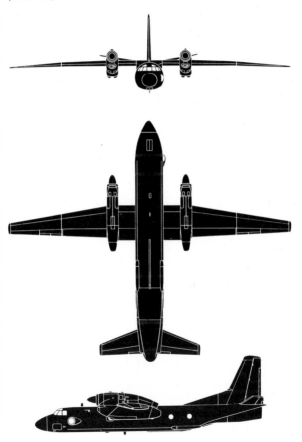

ANTONOV AN-72 (COALER)

Country of Origin: USSR.

Type: STOL utility transport.

Power Plant: Two 14,330 lb st (6500 kgp) Lotarev D-36 turbofans.

Performance: Max speed, 472 mph (760 km/h); max continuous cruise, 447 mph (720 km/h); normal operating altitudes, 26,250-32,800 ft (8000–10000 m); range with 30 min reserves (max fuel), 2,360 mls (3800 km), (max payload), 620 mls (1000 km).

Weights: Max take-off, 72,750 lb (33000 kg).

Accommodation: Flight crew of three and provision for up to 32 passengers on fold-down seats along cabin sides, or 24 casualty stretchers plus medical attendant.

Status: First of two protypes flown 31 August 1977, these subsequently serving as development aircraft for a refined series version, the An-74, flown early in 1984.

Notes: The An-72 and its production derivative, the An-74, achieve short take-off and landing characteristics (STOL) by means of upper surface blowing, engine exhaust gases flowing over the upper wing surfaces and the inboard slotted flaps. The series An-74, of which few details had been revealed at the time of closing for press, has similar D-36 turbofans and is essentially a refined version of the An-72, having an extended span and a wheel-ski undercarriage permitting operation on snow and ice landing strips. Maximum take-off weight is quoted as some 6,614 lb (3000 kg) less than that of the An-72, and maximum payload as 16,535 lb (7500 kg) as compared with 22,045 lb (10000 kg).

ANTONOV AN-72 (COALER)

Dimensions: Span, 84 ft 9 in (25,83 m); length, 87 ft 2½ in (26,58 m); height, 27 ft 0¼ in (8,23 m); wing area, 969 sq ft (90 000 m²).

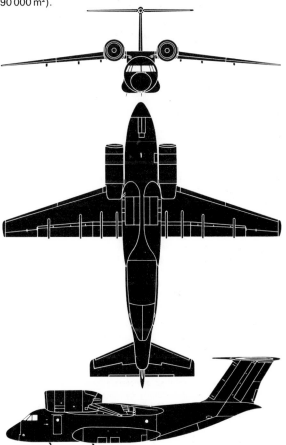

ANTONOV AN-124 RUSLAN (CONDOR)

Country of Origin: USSR.
Type: Heavy strategic freighter.
Power Plant: Four 51,650 lb st (23 430 kgp) Lotarev D-18T turbofans.
Performance: Cruising speed, 497–528 mph (800–850 km/h) at 32,810–39,370 ft (10 000–12 000 m); range (max payload of 330,688 lb/150 000 kg), 2,796 mls (4 500 km), (max fuel), 10,250 mls (16 500 km).
Weights: Max take-off, 892,857 lb (405 000 kg).
Accommodation: Flight crew of six and upper deck accommodation for relief crews and up to 88 personnel. The lower deck can reportedly accommodate all elements of the SS-20 mobile intermediate-range ballistic missile systems and the largest Soviet tanks and armoured personnel carriers.
Status: The first of three prototypes was flown on 26 December 1982, series production being initiated during the course of 1984.
Notes: Scheduled to complete its development programme mid-1986, the An-124 Ruslan (a character in Russian folklore possessing unusual size and strength) has been developed to meet a mid 'seventies requirement for an aircraft capable of lifting a 150-*tonne* payload over a normal range of 4 500 km (2,796 mls) and operating with minimum support from semi-prepared or frozen airstrips of the order of 1 200 m (1,312 yds) in length. During the course of 1985, the An-124 lifted a 171 219-kg (377,466-lb) payload to an altitude of 10 750 m (35 270 ft) to establish a new international record. The flight control system is entirely fly-by-wire, 12,125 lb (5 500 kg) of carbon composites and glassfibre materials are incorporated in the aircraft, and the freight hold is partially pressurised in flight. The visor-type nose is raised over the flight deck to provide direct forward access to the hold.

ANTONOV AN-124 RUSLAN (CONDOR)

Dimensions: Span, 240 ft 6 in (73,30 m); length, 228 ft 0 in (69,50 m).

ARV SUPER2

Country of Origin: United Kingdom.

Type: Side-by-side two-seat light trainer and tourer.

Power Plant: One 77 bhp Hewland Engineering three-cylinder two-stroke engine.

Performance: Max speed, 125 mph (202 km/h); econ cruise, 100 mph (161 km/h); max climb, 800 ft/min (4 m/sec).

Weights: Empty, 635 lb (288 kg); max take-off, 1,045 lb (474 kg).

Status: First of two prototypes flown on 11 March 1985, with certification scheduled for early 1986. Initial aircraft are to be provided in (65% complete) kit form, the Super 2 subsequently being offered in complete form. Twenty orders recorded by beginning of 1986.

Notes: Designed and built by ARV Aviation, the Super2 is relatively conventional in appearance, but is innovative in the use in its construction of superplastically-formed alumium alloy pressings which make possible double curvature for improved styling. Claimed to offer operational costs of approximately half those of the most widely-used two-seat light trainers, such as the Cessna 152, and an appreciably lower initial purchase price, the Super 2 is initially being marketed in kit form under the auspices of the Popular Flying Association, a production run of 60 kits being foreseen for 1986. Features include removable wings to facilitate road transportation.

ARV SUPER2

Dimensions: Span, 28 ft 6 in (8,69 m); length, 18 ft 0 in (5,49 m); wing area, 92 sq ft (8,55 m²).

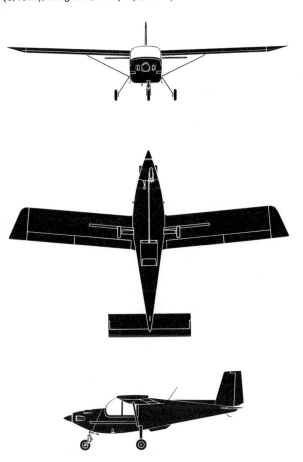

AVTEK 400

Country of Origin: USA.

Type: Light corporate transport.

Power Plant: Two 750 shp Pratt & Whitney Canada PT6A-135M turboprops.

Performance: (Estimated) Max cruising speed, 415 mph (668 km/h) at 25,000 ft (7 620 m); initial climb, 5,020 ft/min (25,5 m/sec); ceiling, 42,500 ft (12 955 m); max range, 2,395 mls (3 855 km) at econ cruise.

Weights: Empty equipped, 3,728 lb (1 691 kg); max take-off, 6,000 lb (2 722 kg).

Accommodation: Pilot and co-pilot/passenger on flight deck and optional arrangements for four to eight passengers in main cabin.

Status: Proof-of-concept aircraft flown 17 September 1984, and first of two flight test aircraft (definitive configuration) scheduled to fly September 1986, with certification anticipated July 1987.

Notes: The Avtek 400 is constructed virtually entirely of composite materials, predominantly Du Pont Kevlar skin over a Nomex honeycomb. The proof-of-concept aircraft (illustrated above) differs in a number of respects from the definitive model (illustrated opposite), although the fundamental configuration has remained unchanged. The overall length has been increased by 5·4 ft (1·64 m), 15·5 deg of sweepback has been applied to the wing, the positive dihedral of which has given place to two deg of anhedral, and the span of the foreplane has been increased some 3 ft (90 cm). The leading edge wing roots have been extended forward to increase fuel capacity, the areas of both main wing and foreplane have been reduced and fuselage diameter has been increased. The Finnish Valmet concern has acquired the rights to build military versions for surveillance, patrol and early warning.

AVTEK 400

Dimensions: Span, 34 ft 5⅓ in (10,50 m); length, 39 ft 4½ in (12,00 m); height, 10 ft 9 in (3,27 m); wing area, 143·16 sq ft (13,30 m²).

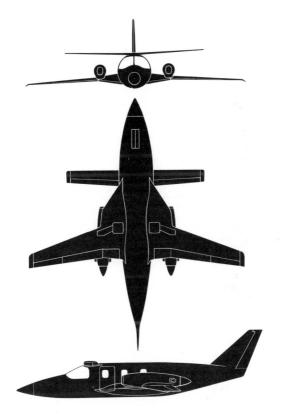

BEECHCRAFT 1900C

Country of Origin: USA.

Type: Regional commercial transport and convertible passenger/freight transport.

Power Plant: Two 1,100 shp Pratt & Whitney Canada PT6A-65B turboprops.

Performance: Max cruising speed (at 14,000 lb/6 350 kg), 295 mph (474 km/h) at 8,000 ft (2 440 m), 291 mph (468 km/h) at 16,000 ft (4 875 m), 271 mph (435 km/h) at 25,000 ft (7 620 m); max initial climb, 2,330 ft/min (11,84 m/sec); range (with max fuel and 45 min reserves) at max cruise power, 611 mls (984 km) at 8,000 ft (2 440 m), 913 mls (1 469 km) at 25,000 ft (7 620 m), at max range power, 686 mls (1 104 km) at 8,000 ft (2 440 m), 914 mls (1 471 km) at 25,000 ft (7 620 m).

Weights: Empty, 8,700 lb (3 946 kg); max take-off, 16,600 lb (7 530 kg).

Accommodation: Flight crew of two and standard seating for 19 passengers in individual seats two abreast with central aisle. Various corporate transport arrangements available with typical seating for eight to 14 passengers. With the latter arrangement six seats are accommodated by a forward cabin and eight by an aft cabin.

Status: First of three prototypes flown on 3 September 1982, with certification following on 22 November 1983. Standard production model (1900C) embodies upward-hinging cargo door and entered service (with Bar Harbour) in February 1984, 30 being delivered during that year, with production continuing at one to one-and-a-half monthly at end of 1985.

Notes: The Beechcraft 1900C shares some 40 per cent component part commonality with the King Air 200.

BEECHCRAFT 1900C

Dimensions: Span, 54 ft 6 in (16,61 m); length, 57 ft 10 in (17,63 m); height, 14 ft 10¾ in (4,53 m); wing area, 303 sq ft (28,15 m²).

BEECHCRAFT 2000 STARSHIP I

Country of Origin: USA.

Type: Light corporate executive transport.

Power Plant: Two 1,000 shp Pratt & Whitney Canada PT6A-27 turboprops.

Performance: (Estimated) Max cruising speed, 403 mph (648 km/h) at 25,000 ft (7 620 m); econ cruise, 316 mph (508 km/h) at 39,000 ft (11 885 m); max initial climb, 3,248 ft/min (16,50 m/sec); service ceiling, 41,000 ft (12 495 m); range with 45 min reserves (max fuel), 3,014 mls (4 850 km) at long-range cruise, (max payload) 1,298 mls (2 090 km).

Weights: (Estimated) Empty equipped, 8,011 lb (3 634 kg); max take-off, 12,500 lb (5 670 kg).

Accommodation: Provision for two crew on flight deck and max of 10 passengers in main cabin. Six basic interior configurations, a typical arrangement providing seven single seats and a two-place divan.

Status: An 85 per cent scale proof-of-concept vehicle was first flown on 29 August 1983, the first of three full-scale prototypes (NC-1) was scheduled to fly February 1986, with the second (NC-2) and third (NC-3) following at four-week and eight-week intervals respectively. Certification is anticipated late 1986 or early 1987, with customer deliveries commencing during the course of 1987.

Notes: Making extensive use of such materials as boron, carbon, Kevlar and glassfibre in its structure, the Starship is innovative in concept in mating an aft-mounted laminar-flow wing with a variable-sweep foreplane. The sweep of the latter is changed with flap extension to provide fully automatic pitch-trim compensation. The scaled proof-of-concept vehicle was developed and built by Scaled Composites Incorporated.

BEECHCRAFT 2000 STARSHIP I

Dimensions: Span, 54 ft 6½ in (16,62 m); length, 46 ft 1 in (14,05 m); height, 12 ft 11 in (3,94 m); wing area, 280·9 sq ft (26,09 m²).

BOEING 737-300

Country of Origin: USA.

Type: Short-haul commercial airliner.

Power Plant: Two 20,000 lb st (9 072 kgp) General Electric CFM56-3-B1 turbofans.

Performance: Max cruising speed, 558 mph (899 km/h) at 25,000 ft (7 620 m); econ cruise, 489 mph (787 km/h) at 35,000 ft (10 670 m); range cruise, 495 mph (797 km/h) at 35,000 ft (10 670 m); max range at econ cruise (max payload), 2,625 mls (4 225 km), (max fuel), 3,408 mls (5 485 km).

Weights: Operational empty, 69,580 lb (31 561 kg); max take-off, 135,000 lb (61 236 kg).

Accommodation: Flight crew of two and alternative arrangements for 110 to 149 passengers, typical arrangements including mixed class with four-abreast seating for eight first class and six-abreast seating for 114 or 120 tourist class passengers, or one class arrangement for 132, 140 or 149 tourist class passengers.

Status: First Model 737-300 flown on 24 February 1984, with second on 2 March 1984. First customer delivery (to US Air) 28 November 1984, and total of 411 ordered by beginning of December 1985, when 1,532 of all models of the Model 737 had been ordered and production was being increased from 11 to 14 aircraft monthly.

Notes: The Model 737-300 differs from the -200 (see 1983 edition) in having new engines, a 104-in (2,64-m) overall "stretch", strengthened wings and modified wingtips. The -300 is not simply a stretched and re-engined version of the Model 737 as it embodies many of the developments made available by the Model 757 and 767 programmes, and it is seen as complementary to the Model 737-200.

BOEING 737-300

Dimensions: Span, 94 ft 9 in (28,90 m); length, 109 ft 7 in (33,40 m); height, 36 ft 6 in (11,12 m); wing area, 980 sq ft (91,04 m²).

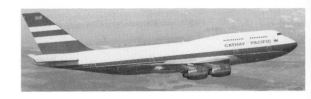

BOEING 747-300

Country of Origin: USA.

Type: Long-haul commercial airliner.

Power Plant: Four 54,750 lb st (24 835 kgp) Pratt & Whitney JT9D-7R4G2 turbofans.

Performance: Max cruise speed, 583 mph (939 km/h) at 35,000 ft (10 670 m); econ cruise, 564 mph (907 km/h) at 35,000 ft (10 670 m); long-range cruise, 558 mph (898 km/h); range (max payload at econ cruise), 6,860 mls (11 040 km), (max fuel at long-range cruise), 8,606 mls (13 850 km).

Weights: Operational empty, 389,875 lb (176 847 kg); max take-off, 833,000 lb (377 850 kg).

Accommodation: Normal flight crew of three and up to 69 passengers six-abreast on upper deck, plus basic mixed-class arrangement for 410 passengers, or 415 passengers nine-abreast or 484 10-abreast in economy class seating.

Status: First Model 747-300 flown on 5 October 1982, with first customer delivery (Swissair) March 1983. Total of 671 of all versions of the Model 747 ordered by the beginning of December 1985, with 634 delivered and production running at two per month.

Notes: The Model 747-300 differs from the -200 primarily in having a 23-ft (7,0-m) lengthening of the upper deck affording a (typical) 10 per cent increase in total accommodation. Boeing is offering to convert existing Model 747s to -300 standard. The first Model 747-100 was flown on 9 February 1969, and the first Model 747-200 on 11 October 1970. On 22 October 1985, a launch order was announced for 10 of the Model 747-400. The -400, which will enter test in the first quarter of 1988, will use 56,000 lb st (25 400 kgp) PW4000 or CF6-80C2 engines and will have a gross weight of up to 850,000 lb (385 560 kg). It will feature extended wingtips and winglets, a two-crew flight deck and make extensive use of new materials.

BOEING 747-300

Dimensions: Span, 195 ft 8 in (59,64 m); length, 231 ft 4 in (70,51 m); height, 63 ft 5 in (19,33 m); wing area, 5,685 sq ft (528,15 m²).

41

BOEING 757-200

Country of Origin: USA.

Type: Short/medium-haul commercial airliner.

Power Plant: Two 37,500 lb st (17 010 kgp) Rolls-Royce RB.211-535C, 38,200 lb st (17 327 kgp) Pratt & Whitney 2037 or 40,100 lb st (18 190 kgp) Rolls-Royce RB.211-535E4 turbofans.

Performance: (RB.211-535C engines) Max cruise speed, 570 mph (917 km/h) at 30,000 ft (9145 m); econ cruise, 528 mph (850 km/h) at 39,000 ft (11 885 m); range (max payload), 2,210 mls (3 556 km) at econ cruise, (max fuel), 5,343 mls (8 598 km) at long-range cruise.

Weights: Operational empty, 128,450 lb (58 265 kg); max take-off (RB.211-535C engines), 220,000 lb (99 790 kg).

Accommodation: Flight crew of two (with provision for optional third crew member) and typical arrangement of 178 mixed class or 196 tourist class passengers, with max single-class seating for 239 passengers.

Status: First Model 757 flown on 19 February 1982, with first customer deliveries (to Eastern) December 1982 and (British Airways) January 1983. Orders totalling 156 aircraft by December 1985, with deliveries with Pratt & Whitney engines having commenced (to Delta Air Lines) October 1984. Production rate of two-and-a-half aircraft monthly at beginning of 1986, with total of 80 delivered.

Notes: Two versions of the Model 757 are currently on offer, one with a max take-off weight of 220,000 lb (99 790 kg) and the other with a max take-off weight of 240,000 lb (108 864 kg). The Model 757 is of narrowbody configuration and its wing has been optimised for short-haul routes. At the beginning of 1986, Boeing was engaged in studies of a combi version with a rear freight door, and a freighter and a convertible, both with forward freight doors.

BOEING 757-200

Dimensions: Span, 124 ft 6 in (37,82 m); length, 155 ft 3 in (47,47 m); height, 44 ft 6 in (13,56 m); wing area, 1,951 sq ft (181,25 m²).

BOEING 767-200

Country of Origin: USA.

Type: Medium-haul commercial airliner.

Power Plant: Two 48,000 lb st (21 773 kgp) Pratt & Whitney JT9D-7R4D or General Electric CF6-80A turbofans.

Performance: (JT9D-7R4D engines) Max cruise speed, 556 mph (895 km/h) at 39,000 ft (11 890 m); econ cruise, 528 mph (850 km/h) at 39,000 ft (11 890 m); range (with max payload and no reserves), 2,717 mls (4 373 km) at econ cruise, (max fuel) 6,680 mls (10 750 km).

Weights: (JT9D-7R4D engines) Operational empty, 179,580 lb (81 457 kg); max take-off, 300,000 lb (136 080 kg).

Accommodation: Flight crew of two (with optional three-crew arrangement) and typical mixed-class seating for 18 six-abreast and 193 seven-abreast with two aisles, with max single-class seating for 290 passengers eight-abreast.

Status: First Model 767 (JT9D-7R4D engines) flown on 26 September 1981, (CF6-80A engines) 19 February 1982. First customer delivery (to United) on 18 August 1982, and 123 delivered by December 1985, when 193 were on order.

Notes: Three basic versions of the Model 767 were on offer at the beginning of 1986 with 300,000 lb (136 080 kg), 315,000 lb (142 884 kg) and 335,000 lb (151 956 kg) max. take-off weights, the last-mentioned version having 50,000 lb st (22 680 kg) CF6-80A2 engines and a max volume payload range of 4,000 mls (6 437 km). Several variants are under development, including a stretched model, the 767-300 with a fuselage lengthened by 21 ft 1 in (6,43 m) and deliveries (to Japan Air Lines) to commence September 1986, and a freighter, weights up to 360,000 lb (163 296 kg) being possible with the present wing and 55,000 lb st (24 948 kgp) engines. The longer-range 767-200ER has been ordered by Ethiopian Airlines, Japan Air Lines, Air Canada, Qantas and the Egyptian government, with first delivery (to Ethiopian) in May 1984.

BOEING 767-200

Dimensions: Span, 156 ft 4 in (47,65 m); length, 159 ft 2 in (48,50 m); height, 52 ft 0 in (15,85 m); wing area, 3,050 sq ft (283,3 m²).

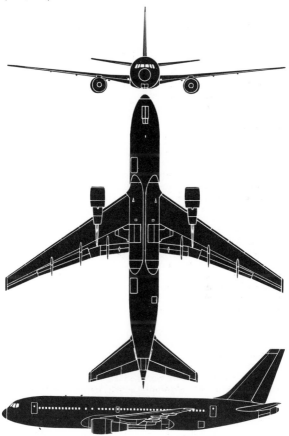

BOEING E-3 SENTRY

Country of Origin: USA.

Type: Airborne warning and control system aircraft.

Power Plant: Four 21,000 lb st (9 525 kgp) Pratt & Whitney TF33-PW-100A turbofans.

Performance: (At max weight) Average cruise speed, 479 mph (771 km/h) at 28,900-40,100 ft (8 810-12 220 m); average loiter speed, 376 mph (605 km/h) at 29,000 ft (8 840 m); time on station (unrefuelled) at 1,150 mls (1 850 km) from base, 6 hrs, (with one refuelling), 14·4 hrs; ferry range, 5,034 mls (8 100 km) at 475 mph (764 km/h).

Weights: Empty, 170,277 lb (77 238 kg); normal loaded, 214,300 lb (97 206 kg); max take-off, 325,000 lb (147 420 kg).

Accommodation: Operational crew of 17 comprising flight crew of four, systems maintenance team of four, a battle commander and an air defence team of eight.

Status: First of two (EC-137D) development aircraft flown 9 February 1972, two pre-production E-3As following in 1975. First 24 delivered to USAF as E-3As have been modified to E-3B standards, and final 10 (including updated third test aircraft) were delivered as E-3Cs. Eighteen were delivered (in similar configuration to E-3C) to NATO as E-3As with completion April 1985. Five CFM56-powered aircraft being delivered to Saudi Arabia between August 1985 and March 1987.

Notes: Aircraft initially delivered to USAF as E-3As have now been fitted with JTIDS (Joint Tactical Information Distribution System), ECM-resistant voice communications, additional HF and UHF radios, austere maritime surveillance capability and more situation display consoles as E-3Bs. The E-3C featured most E-3B modifications at the production stage.

BOEING E-3 SENTRY

Dimensions: Span, 145 ft 9 in (44,42 m); length, 152 ft 11 in (46,61 m); height, 42 ft 5 in (12,93 m); wing area, 2,892 sq ft (268,67 m²).

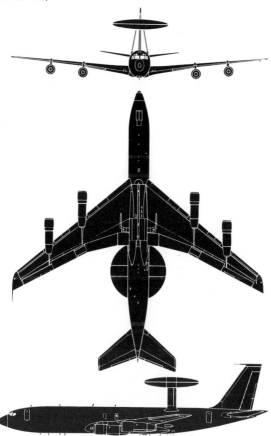

BRITISH AEROSPACE 125-800

Country of Origin: United Kingdom.
Type: Light corporate executive transport.
Power Plant: Two 4,300 lb st (1 950 kgp) Garrett TFE731-5R-1H turbofans.
Performance: Max cruising speed, 533 mph (858 km/h) at 29,000 ft (8 840 m); econ cruise, 461 mph (741 km/h) at 39,000–43,000 ft (11 900–13 100 m); max initial climb, 3,100 ft/min (15,75 m/sec); service ceiling, 43,000 ft (13 100 m); range (max payload), 3,305 mls (5 318 km), (max fuel with VFR reserves), 3,454 mls (5 560 km).
Weights: Operational empty (typical), 15,120 lb (6 858 kg); max take-off, 27,400 lb (12 430 kg).
Accommodation: Pilot and co-pilot on flight deck with seat for third crew member, and standard arrangement for eight passengers in main cabin with optional arrangements for up to 14 seats.
Status: Prototype of 800 series 125 flown on 26 May 1983, with type certification being achieved in May 1984. Production rate was two per month during 1985, 42 800 series aircraft having been sold by November of that year.
Notes: The BAe 125-800 is an extensively revised development of the -700 (see 1982 edition) with more powerful engines, new, longer-span outboard wing sections, new ailerons, redesigned flight deck and larger ventral fuel tank. A total of 573 of the earlier turbojet- and turbofan-powered models was sold, including 215 -700s. The availability of an optional aft baggage pannier and thrust reversers was announced during 1985.

BRITISH AEROSPACE 125-800

Dimensions: Span, 51 ft 4½ in (15,66 m); length, 51 ft 2 in (15,59 m); height, 17 ft 7 in (5,37 m); wing area, 374 sq ft (32,75 m²).

BRITISH AEROSPACE 146-200

Country of Origin: United Kir.gdom.

Type: Short-haul regional airliner.

Power Plant: Four 6,968 lb st (3 160 kgp) Avco Lycoming ALF 502R-5 turbofans.

Performance: Max cruise speed, 483 mph (778 km/h) at 26,000 ft (7 925 m); econ cruise, 441 mph (710 km/h) at 30,000 ft (9 145 m); long-range cruise, 436 mph (702 km/h) at 30,000 ft (9 145 m); range (max payload), 1,232 mls (1 982 km) at econ cruise, (max fuel), 1,440 mls (2 317 km), or (with optional fuel capacity), 1,727 mls (2 780 km).

Weights: Operational empty, 48,500 lb (22 000 kg); max take-off, 89,500 lb (40 597 kg).

Accommodation: Flight crew of two and maximum seating (single-class) for 106 passengers six-abreast.

Status: First BAe 146-100 flown 3 September 1981, and first BAe 146-200 flown on 1 August 1982, with first customer deliveries of -100 (Dan Air) early 1983, and -200 (Air Wisconsin) March 1983. Sixty-one BAe 146s ordered by beginning of December 1985, plus 30 on option, and 34 aircraft delivered.

Notes: The BAe 146 is currently being manufactured in -100 form with an 85 ft 10 in (26,16 m) fuselage for up to 82 passengers and -200 form (described and illustrated). Apart from fuselage length and capacity, the two versions of the BAe 146 are similar in all respects, but the uprated R-5 version of the ALF 502 turbofan is available for the longer -200 model which is featured by most initial orders. The BAe 146-300, which is expected to fly in 1987, will feature a 10 ft 6 in (3,20 m) fuselage stretch to provide accommodation for 122–134 passengers. It will be powered by 7,500 lb st (3 402 kgp) ALF 502R-7 engines, will feature wingtip fences and will be delivered from early 1988.

BRITISH AEROSPACE 146-200

Dimensions: Span, 85 ft 5 in (26,34 m); length, 93 ft 8$\frac{1}{2}$ in (28,56 m); height, 28 ft 3 in (8,61 m); wing area, 832 sq ft (77,30 m²).

BRITISH AEROSPACE ATP

Country of Origin: United Kingdom.

Type: Regional commercial transport.

Power Plant: Two 2,150 shp (2,400 shp emergency) Pratt & Whitney Canada PW124 or (2,500 shp emergency) PW125 turboprops.

Performance: (Estimated) Max cruising speed, 306 mph (492 km/h) at 15,000 ft (4 670 m); econ cruise, 301 mph (485 km/h) at 18,000 ft (5 485 m); initial climb, 1,370 ft/min (6,96 m/sec); max operating altitude, 25,000 ft (7 620 m); range (with 64 passengers), 1,134 mls (1 825 km); max range (with 8,000-lb/3 629-kg payload), 2,073 mls (3 335 km).

Weights: Typical operational empty, 29,970 lb (13 594 kg); max take-off, 49,500 lb (22 453 kg).

Accommodation: Flight crew of two and 64–68 passengers in four-abreast seating.

Status: Prototype scheduled to enter flight test on 6 August 1986, with second aircraft (for eventual commercial sale) following approx six weeks later for certification flying expected to be completed 30 July 1987, followed immediately by first customer delivery (to British Midland Airways). Anticipated production tempo of two monthly. The launch customers are British Midland Airways with three on order and two on option, and Leeward Island Air Transport (LIAT) with two on order and two on option

Notes: The ATP (initials signifying "Advanced Turboprop") is technically a derivative of the BAe 748 embodying fuselage stretch, new engines, systems and equipment, swept vertical tail surfaces and a redesigned nose. The ATP features slow-running six-bladed composite-construction propellers, and its most direct competitor from the capacity viewpoint will be the ATR 72.

BRITISH AEROSPACE ATP

Dimensions: Span, 100 ft 6 in (30,63 m); length, 85 ft 4 in (26,01 m); height, 23 ft 5 in (7,14 m); wing area, 842·84 sq ft (78,30 m²).

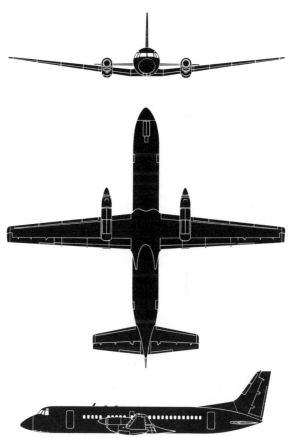

BRITISH AEROSPACE EAP

Country of Origin: United Kingdom.
Type: Single-seat advanced fighter technology demonstrator.
Power Plant: Two (approx) 9,000 lb st (4 082 kgp) dry and 17,000 lb st (7 711 kgp) reheat Turbo-Union RB199–34R Mk 104 turbofans.
Performance: (Estimated) Max speed, 1,320 mph (2 124 km/h) plus or Mach=2·0 plus above 36,000 ft (10 975 m). No further details available for publication.
Weights: No details available.
Armament: (Typical) Four BAe Sky Flash AAMs (two beneath fuselage and two beneath wing roots) and two AIM-9L Sidewinder AAMs (at wingtips).
Status: Single example scheduled to enter flight test in May 1986.
Notes: The EAP (Experimental Aircraft Programme) is intended to demonstrate three basic new technologies that it is proposed to incorporate in the planned EFA (European Fighter Aircraft) which is to be developed jointly by the UK, Federal Germany, Italy and Spain. These are advanced structural design, including extensive use of carbonfibre composites; active fly-by-wire controls to achieve extreme agility and an advanced electronic cockpit. The EAP has been designed to demonstrate a complete weapon system meeting a generally similar requirement to the EFA, and it is anticipated that the aircraft will be utilised for weapon system trials. The EAP is a collaborative venture in that the design of the wing has been shared with Aeritalia of Italy and German companies are participating in the avionics. The EAP makes interesting comparison with the French Rafale (pages 84–85) which was conceived with essentially similar aims.

BRITISH AEROSPACE EAP

Dimensions: Span, 36 ft 7¾ in (11,17 m); length, 48 ft 2¾ in (14,70 m); wing area, 560 sq ft (52,00 m²).

BRITISH AEROSPACE HARRIER GR MK 5

Country of Origin: United Kingdom and USA.

Type: Single-seat V/STOL close support and tactical reconnaissance aircraft.

Power Plant: One 21,750 lb st (9 866 kgp) Rolls-Royce Pegasus Mk 105 vectored-thrust turbofan.

Performance: Max speed (clean aircraft), 668 mph
(1 075 km/h) or Mach = 0·88 at sea level, 614 mph (988 km/
h) or Mach = 0·93 at 36,000 ft (10 970 m); tactical radius (interdiction with seven 1,000-lb/453,6-kg bombs and two 25
-mm cannon), 692 mls (1 114 km) HI-LO-HI; ferry range (with
four 250 Imp gal/1 136 l drop tanks), 2,876 mls (4 630 km).

Weights: Operational empty, 12,750 lb (5 783 kg); max
take-off (for VTO), 19,185 lb (8 702 kg), (for STO) 29,750 lb
(13 495 kg).

Armament: Two 25-mm Aden cannon and up to 9,200 lb
(4 173 kg) of ordnance on one fuselage centreline and six
wing hardpoints.

Status: First of two (weapon system) development aircraft
flown on 30 April 1985, with first deliveries to the RAF scheduled to commence in 1987 against initial requirement for 60,
with production stablising at two per month.

Notes: The Harrier GR Mk 5 is the RAF equivalent of the US
Marine Corps' AV-8B Harrier II, the airframe of both models
being split between British Aerospace and McDonnell Douglas on a 50-50 basis in the case of the Harrier GR Mk 5 and
40-60 in the case of the AV-8B. The USMC has a requirement
for 328 AV-8Bs of which some 28 will be supplied as tandem
two-seat TAV-8B trainers. Twelve AV-8Bs are to be supplied
to the Spanish Navy. The RAF anticipates achieving operational capability with the Harrier GR Mk 5 by early to mid
1988.

BRITISH AEROSPACE HARRIER GR MK 5

Dimensions: Span, 30 ft 4 in (9,24 m); length, 46 ft 4 in (14,12 m); height, 11 ft 7¾ in (3,55 m); wing area, 238·4 sq ft (22,15 m²).

BRITISH AEROSPACE HAWK 200

Country of Origin: United Kingdom.
Type: Single-seat multi-role light fighter.
Power Plant: One (prototype) 5,700 lb st (2 585 kgp)
Rolls-Royce Turboméca Adour 861 or (series) 5,850 lb st
(2 654 kgp) Adour 871 turbofan.
Performance: (Estimated with Adour 871) Max speed,
645 mph (1 038 km/h) at sea level of Mach = 0·846; service
ceiling, 50,000 ft (15 250 m); tactical radius HI-LO-HI (with
5,000 lb/2 268-kg warload), 622 mls (1 000 kg), LO-LO-LO
(with 6,000-lb/2 722-kg warload), 155 mls (250 km); ferry
range (with two 190 Imp gal/860 l external tanks), 2,533 mls
(4 080 km).
Weights: Empty, 8,750 lb (3 969 kg); max take-off, 19,000 lb
(8 620 kg).
Armament: Two 27-mm IWKA-Mauser or two 25-mm Aden
cannon and max external load of 6,800 lb (3 100 kg) distributed between seven external stores stations.
Status: Prototype scheduled to fly May 1986.
Notes: The Hawk 200 is a dedicated combat derivative of the
Hawk two-seat basic/advanced trainer and light tactical aircraft (see 1985 edition) and embodying much of the development work for the private-venture two-seat Hawk 100 which
features an inertial navigator, head-up display, laser rangefin-
der and weapon aiming computer. The redesigned forward
fuselage accommodates radar, but the single-seater retains
some 80 per cent commonality with the two-seater. The first
of 175 two-seat Hawks for the RAF was flown on 19 May
1975, versions having been ordered by Abu Dhabi, Dubai,
Finland, Indonesia, Kenya, Kuwait, Saudi Arabia and Zim-
babwe, and a carrier-capable version, the T-45A Goshawk, is
being developed for the US Navy.

BRITISH AEROSPACE HAWK 200

Dimensions: Span, 30 ft 9¾ in (9,39 m); length, 36 ft 3 in (11,05 m); Height, 13 ft 1 in (4,00 m); wing area, 179·64 sq ft (16,69 m²).

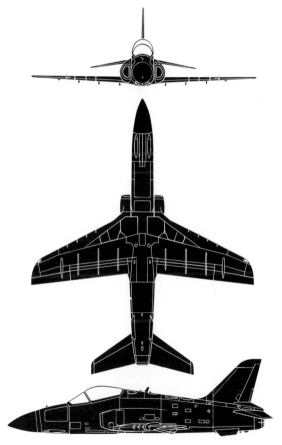

BRITISH AEROSPACE JETSTREAM 31

Country of Origin: United Kingdom.

Type: Light corporate transport and regional airliner.

Power Plant: Two 900 shp Garrett TPE 331-10 turboprops.

Performance: Max cruise speed, 299 mph (482 km/h) at 20,000 ft (6 100 m); long-range cruise, 265 mph (426 km/h) at 25,000 ft (7 620 m); initial climb, 2,200 ft/min (11,2 m/sec); max range (with 19 passengers and IFR reserves), 737 mls (1 186 km), (with 12 passengers), 1,094 mls (1 760 km), (with nine passengers), 1,324 mls (2 130 km).

Weights: Empty equipped (including flight crew), 8,840 lb (4 010 kg); max take-off, 14,550 lb (6 600 kg).

Accommodation: Two seats side by side on flight deck with basic corporate executive seating for eight passengers, with optional 12-seat executive shuttle arrangement, or up to 19 passengers three-abreast with offset aisle in high-density regional airline arrangement.

Status: First Jetstream 31 flown on 18 March 1982, following flight development aircraft (converted from a Series 1 airframe) flown on 28 March 1980. First customer delivery (Contactair of Stuttgart) made 15 December 1982. Jetstream 31 sales commitments totalled 97 aircraft by December 1985. Production tempo is being increased from 36 to 48 aircraft annually during the course of 1986.

Notes: The Jetstream 31 is a derivative of the Handley Page H.P.137 Jetstream, the original prototype of which was flown on 18 August 1967. Most Jetstreams sold have been the basic "Commuter" configured model with 18 passenger seats (increased to 19 by removal of the toilet compartment). Four aircraft have been ordered by the Royal Navy for observer training as Jetstream T Mk 3s with ASR 360 radar.

BRITISH AEROSPACE JETSTREAM 31

Dimensions: Span, 52 ft 0 in (15,85 m); length, 47 ft 2 in (14,37 m); height, 17 ft 6 in (5,37 m); wing area, 270 sq ft (25,08 m²).

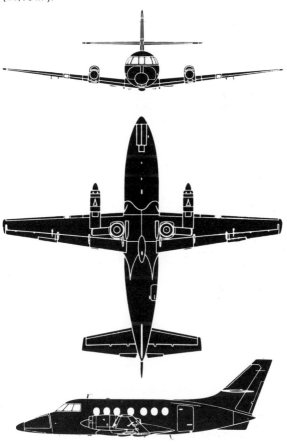

BRITISH AEROSPACE NIMROD AEW MK 3

Country of Origin: United Kingdom.
Type: Airborne warning and control system aircraft.
Power Plant: Four 12,160 lb st (5 515 kgp) Rolls-Royce RB.168-20 Spey Mk 250 turbofans.
Performance: No details have been released for publication, but maximum and transit speeds are likely to be generally similar to those of the MR Mk 2 (see 1984 edition), and maximum endurance is in excess of 10 hours. The mission requirement calls for 6–7 hours on station at 29,000-35,000 ft (8 840-10 670 m) at approx 350 mph (563 km/h) at 750-1,000 miles (1 120-1 600 km) from base.
Weights: Max take-off (approx), 190,000 lb (85 185 kg).
Accommodation: Flight crew of four and tactical team of six, latter comprising tactical air control officer, communications control officer, EWSM (Electronic Warfare Support Measures) operator and three air direction officers.
Status: Total of 11 Nimrod MR Mk 1 airframes have been rebuilt to AEW Mk 3 standard of which fully representative prototype flew on 16 July 1980. The Nimrod AEW Mk 3 is now expected to enter service with the RAF during 1987 with interim capability, five aircraft having been equipped with mission system avionics by late 1985, but full operational capability is not expected before 1988-9.
Notes: The Nimrod AEW Mk 3 is equipped with Marconi mission system avionics with identical radar aerials mounted in nose and tail, these being synchronised and each sequentially sweeping through 180 deg in azimuth in order to provide uninterrupted coverage throughout the 360 deg of combined sweep. EWSM pods are located at the wingtips and weather radar in the starboard wing pinion tank. The Nimrod AEW Mk 3 is intended to provide complementary capability with the Boeing E-3A Sentries operated by the NATO combined force (excluding the UK).

BRITISH AEROSPACE NIMROD AEW MK 3

Dimensions: Span, 115 ft 1 in (35,08 m); length, 137 ft 8½ in (41,97 m); height, 35 ft 0 in (10,67 m); wing area, 2,121 sq ft (197,05 m²).

BRITISH AEROSPACE SEA HARRIER

Country of Origin: United Kingdom.
Type: Single-seat V/STOL shipboard multi-role fighter.
Power Plant: One 21,500 lb st (9 760 kgp) Rolls-Royce
Pegasus 104 vectored-thrust turbofan.
Performance: Max speed (clean aircraft), 720 mph
(1 160 km/h) or Mach = 0·95 at 1,000 ft (305 m), 607 mph
(977 km/h) or Mach = 0·92 at 36,000 ft (10 970 m), (with two
AIM-9L AAMs and two Martel ASMs), 598 mph (962 km/h)
or Mach = 0·83 at sea level; combat radius (recce mission with
two 100 Imp gal/455 l drop tanks), 518 mls (520 km); endurance (with two drop tanks for combat air patrol), 1·5 hrs at
115 mls/185 km from ship with three min combat.
Weights: Empty (approx), 13,000 lb (5 897 kg); normal
loaded (STO), 21,700 lb (9 840 kg); max take-off 25,600 lb
(11 612 kg).
Armament: Provision for two 30-mm cannon plus two
AIM-9L Sidewinder AAMs and up to 5,000 lb (2 268 kg) ordnance on five external stations.
Status: First Sea Harrier (built on production tooling) flown
on 20 August 1978, with deliveries against initial 34 ordered
for Royal Navy completed during 1982 when follow-on batch
of 14 aircraft ordered. Further nine ordered 1984 for 1986–88
delivery. Total of 16 (FRS Mk 51) ordered for Indian Navy.
Notes: The Royal Navy's Sea Harrier FRS Mk 1 is a derivative
of the RAF's Harrier GR Mk 3 (see 1982 edition) to operate
from *Invincible*-class through-deck cruisers. During 1984,
contract awarded for a mid-life update of the Sea Harrier as
the FRS Mk 2 involving installation of Blue Vixen pulse doppler radar. redesigned wing tips to provide two additional
missile stations and provision for Hughes AIM-20 missiles.

BRITISH AEROSPACE SEA HARRIER

Dimensions: Span, 25 ft 3 in (7,70 m); length, 47 ft 7 in (14,50 m); height, 12 ft 2 in (3,70 m); wing area, 201·1 sq ft (18,68 m²).

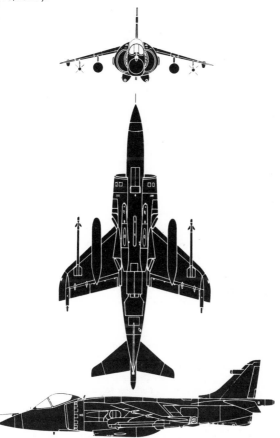

CANADAIR CHALLENGER 601

Country of Origin: Canada.
Type: Light corporate transport.
Power Plant: Two 9,140 lb st (4146 kgp) with 5-min limit or 8,650 lb st (3924 kgp) General Electric CF34-1A turbofans.
Performance: Max cruising speed, 529 mph (851 km/h) or Mach=0·8; normal cruise, 509 mph (819 km/h) or Mach =0·77; range cruise, 488 mph (786 km/h) or Mach=0·74; operational ceiling, 41,000 ft (12 500 m); range (max fuel and IFR reserves), 3,857 mls (6 208 km).
Weights: Empty, 19,950 lb (9 049 kg); operational empty (typical), 25,585 lb (11 605 kg); max take-off, 43,100 lb (19 550 kg).
Accommodation: Flight crew of two on flight deck wiith customer-specified main cabin interiors providing seating for up to 19 passengers.
Status: Prototype Challenger 601 flown on 10 April 1982, with FAA certification following on 25 February 1983. The 100th Challenger (including 81 Challenger 600s) delivered on 19 March 1984, and 42 Challenger 601s delivered by December 1985 when production was one monthly.
Notes: The Challenger 601 is the intercontinental-range derivative of the transcontinental Challenger 600, the latter differing primarily in having 7,500 lb st (3402 kgp) Avco Lycoming ALF 502L turbofans. Production of this version was terminated mid-1983. Two Challengers have been procured by the Canadian Armed Forces and seven have been ordered by the *Luftwaffe*. Late 1985, Canadair offered an upgraded model, the Challenger 3A for delivery commencing spring 1987. This version will have CF34-3A engines of increased thrust, and an advanced navigation and avionics package.

CANADAIR CHALLENGER 601

Dimensions: Span, 64 ft 4 in (19,61 m); length, 68 ft 5 in (20,85 m); height, 20 ft 8 in (6,30 m) wing area (basic), 450 sq ft (41,82 m²).

CASA C-101DD AVIOJET

Country of Origin: Spain.

Type: Tandem two-seat basic/advanced trainer and light tactical support aircraft.

Power Plant: One 4,700 lb st (2130 kgp) Garrett TFE-731-5-1J turbofan.

Performance: (Manufacturer's estimates) Max speed, 518 mph (834 km/h) at 15,000 ft (4570 m), 500 mph (805 km/h) at sea level; max initial climb, 5,300 ft/min (26,92 m/sec); time to 25,000 ft (7620 m), 7·5 min; tactical radius (interdiction with one 30-mm cannon and four 550-lb/250-kg bombs), 345 mls (556 km) LO-LO-LO with 10% reserves; endurance (armed patrol at 115 mls/185 km from base with one 30-mm cannon), 3·5 hrs at 230 mph (370 km/h) at sea level; max range, 2,300 mls (3700 km).

Weights: Empty equipped, 7,716 lb (3500 kg); loaded (training mission), 10,075 lb (4570 kg); max take-off, 13,889 lb (6300 kg).

Armament: One 30-mm cannon or two 12,7-mm machine guns in fuselage pod and up to 4,000 lb (1815 kg) of ordnance on six wing stores stations.

Status: The C-101DD entered flight test in May 1985. First of four Aviojet prototypes flown on 29 June 1977, and 88 (C-101EBs) supplied to Spanish Air Force, four (C-101BBs) to Honduras, and 17 (C-101BBs) and 20 (C-101CCs) are being supplied to Chile, all but the first five being assembled by ENAER.

Notes: The C-101DD is a more powerful and more comprehensively equipped (head-up display, weapon aiming computer, attitude and heading reference system, etc) version of the Aviojet with enhanced attack capability.

CASA C-101 DD AVIOJET

Dimensions: Span, 34 ft 9⅜ in (10,60 m); length, 41 ft 0 in (12,50 m); height, 13 ft 11 in (4,25 m); wing area, 215·3 sq ft (20,00 m²).

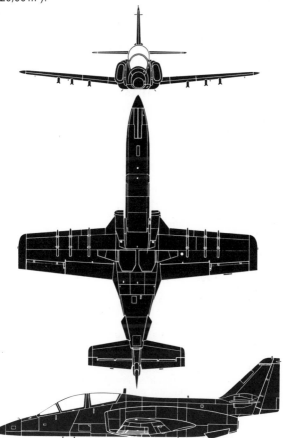

CASA-NURTANIO CN-235

Country of Origin: Spain and Indonesia.
Type: Regional commercial transport, military and civil freighter, and mixed personnel/freight transport.
Power Plant: Two 1,700 shp General Electric CT7-7A turboprops.
Performance: Max cruising speed, 277 mph (446 km/h) at 18,000 ft (5 485 m); long-range cruise, 237 mph (382 km/h) at 18,000 ft (5 485 m); max range (with 44 passengers and IFR reserves), 517 mls (832 km), (with max fuel and 3,748-lb/1 700-kg payload), 2,684 mls (4 320 km).
Weights: Operational empty (freighter), 18,960 lb (8 600 kg), (regional airliner), 20,723 lb (9 400 kg); max take-off, 31,746 lb (14 400 kg).
Accommodation: Flight crew of two and (regional airliner) standard seating arrangements for 40 or 44 passengers four abreast with central aisle.
Status: First prototype flown (in Spain) on 11 November 1983, and second (in Indonesia) on 31 December 1983. Orders claimed at end of 1985 totalled 111 aircraft of which 54 were for the military version. In addition, 46 options were held. Production schedules were uncertain at time of closing for press, but certification was anticipated for early 1986, with customer deliveries commencing soon thereafter.
Notes: The CN-235 is being manufactured jointly by CASA of Spain and Nurtanio of Indonesia on a 50–50 basis without any component production duplication. The bulk of orders have so far been placed with Nurtanio (83) and these include 32 for the Indonesian Air Force and 18 for the Indonesian Navy. Electronic warfare, aeromedical, maritime surveillance and anti-submarine warfare versions are under consideration.

CASA-NURTANIO CN-235

Dimensions: Span, 84 ft 7¾ in (25·81 m); length, 70 ft 0½ in (21,35 m); height, 26 ft 9¾ in (8,17 m); wing area, 636·17 sq ft (59,10 m²).

CESSNA 208 CARAVAN I

Country of Origin: USA.
Type: Light utility transport.
Power Plant: One 600 shp Pratt & Whitney Canada PT6A-114 turboprop.
Performance: Max cruising speed, 214 mph, (345 km/h) at 10,000 ft (3 050 m); initial climb, 1,060 ft/min (5,38 m/sec); time to 10,000 ft (3 050 m), 10 min, to 20,000 ft (6 095 m), 22 min; max range, 1,658 mls (2 668 km).
Weights: Empty, 3,800 lb (1 724 kg); max take-off, 7,300 lb (3 311 kg).
Accommodation: Pilot and up to 13 passengers or useful load of 3,535 lb (1 603 kg). Passenger seating in combination of two and three abreast with aisle between seats.
Status: Engineering prototype flown on 9 December 1982, with first customer delivery (Model 208A) to Federal Express following in February 1985. Production rate of five monthly attained during 1985.
Notes: The Caravan I is claimed to be the first all-new single-turboprop aircraft designed for the utility role to attain production status. Thirty comprising the initial order from Federal Express were of the Model 208A version lacking cabin windows, featuring a ventral cargo pod and having a max take-off weight of 8,000 lb (3 629 kg). Nine more of this version for Federal Express are to be followed by 70 aircraft embodying a 4-ft (1,22-m) fuselage stretch, with deliveries commencing from October 1986. This modified Caravan will have maximum weight increased to 8,700 lb (3 946 kg).

CESSNA 208 CARAVAN I

Dimensions: Span, 52 ft 1¼ in (15,88 m); length, 37 ft 7 in (11,45 m); height, 14 ft 2½ in (4,33 m); wing area, 279·4 sq ft (25,96 m²).

CESSNA 650 CITATION III

Country of Origin: USA.
Type: Light corporate transport.
Power Plant: Two 3,650 lb st (1 656 kgp) Garrett TFE731-3B-100S turbofans.
Performance: Max cruise speed (at 16,000 lb/7 258 kg), 544 mph (875 km/h) at 35,000 ft (10 670 m), 528 mph (850 km/h) at 41,000 ft (12 500 m); time to 35,000 ft (10 670 m) at 20,000 lb (9 072 kg), 14 min; range (with six passengers and 45 min reserve), 3,040 mls (4 894 km) at 482 mph (776 km/h) at 45,000 ft (13 715 m); ferry range, 3,200 mls (5 150 km).
Weights: Operational empty (average), 12,200 lb (5 534 kg); max take-off, 21,000 lb (9 526 kg).
Accommodation: Normal flight crew of two on flight deck and standard main cabin arrangement for six passengers in individual seats.
Status: Two prototypes flown on 30 May 1979 and 2 May 1980 respectively, with certification following on 30 April 1982, and customer deliveries commencing spring 1983. Fifty Citation IIIs were delivered during the course of 1984, the 41st aircraft having been the 1,200th Citation (of all types). Eighty-six had been delivered by December 1985.
Notes: The Citation III owes nothing to preceding Citations despite its name, being of all new aerodynamic design and featuring a supercritical wing. The first production model established two time-to-altitude records in 1983 for aircraft in its class and a record by flying from Gander to Le Bourget in 5 hr 13 min.

CESSNA 650 CITATION III

Dimensions: Span, 53 ft 3½ in (16,30 m); length, 55 ft 6 in (16,90 m); height, 17 ft 3½ in (5,30 m); wing area, 312 sq ft (29,00 m²).

DASSAULT-BREGUET ATLANTIQUE G2 (ATL2)

Country of Origin: France.
Type: Long-range maritime patrol aircraft.
Power Plant: Two 5,665 shp Rolls-Royce/SNECMA Tyne RTy 20 Mk 21 turboprops.
Performance: Max speed, 368 mph (593 km/h) at sea level; normal cruise, 345 mph (556 km/h) at 25,000 ft (7 620 m); typical patrol speed, 196 mph (315 km/h); initial climb, 2,000 ft/min (10,1 m/sec); service ceiling, 30,000 ft (9 100 m); typical mission, 8 hrs patrol at 690 mls (1 110 km) from base at 2,000-3,000 ft (610-915 m); max range, 5,590 mls (9 000 km).
Weights: Empty equipped, 56,217 lb (25 500 kg); normal loaded weight, 97,885 lb (44 400 kg); max take-off, 101,850 lb (46 200 kg).
Accommodation: Normal flight crew of 12, comprising two pilots, flight engineer, forward observer, radio navigator, ESM/ECM/MAD operator, radar operator, tactical co-ordinator, two acoustic operators and two aft observers.
Armament: Up to eight Mk 46 homing torpedoes, nine 550-lb (250-kg) bombs or 12 depth charges, plus two AM 39 Exocet ASMs in forward weapons bay. Four wing stations with combined capacity of 7,715 lb (3 500 kg).
Status: First of two prototypes (converted from ATL1s) flown 8 May 1981, with second following on 26 March 1982, and series production authorised on 24 May 1984 with initial batch of 16 aircraft. Deliveries between 1988 and 1996 to fulfil an *Aéronavale* requirement for 42 aircraft.
Notes: The Atlantic G2 (*Génération* 2), also referred to as the ATL2, is a modernised version of the Atlantic G1 (now referred to as the ATL1), production of which terminated in 1973 after completion of 87 series aircraft.

DASSAULT-BREGUET ATLANTIQUE G2 (ATL2)

Dimensions: Span, 122 ft 7 in (37,36 m); length, 107 ft 0$\frac{1}{4}$ in (36,62 m); height, 37 ft 1$\frac{1}{4}$ in (11,31 m); wing area, 1,295·3 sq ft (120,34 m²).

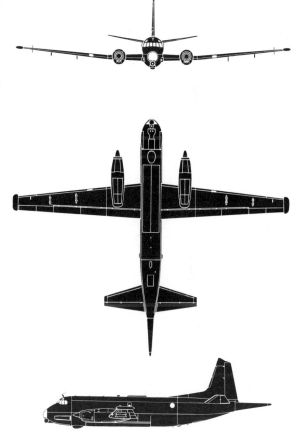

DASSAULT-BREGUET
MYSTERE-FALCON 900

Country of Origin: France.

Type: Light corporate transport.

Power Plant: Three 4,500 lb st (2 040 kgp) Garrett TFE 731-5A turbofans.

Performance: (Estimated) Max cruise, 554 mph (892 km/h) or Mach 0·84 at 39,000 ft (11 890 m); range cruise, 495 mph (797 km/h) or Mach=0·75 at 37,000 ft (11 275 m); range (with eight passengers at long-range cruise with IFR reserves), 4,375 mls (7 040 km), (with 19 passengers), 3,915 mls (6 300 km), (with max payload), 2,765 mls (4 450 km); max cruise altitude, 51,000 ft (15 550 m).

Weights: Operational empty, 23,400 lb (10 615 kg); max take-off, 45,500 lb (20 640 kg).

Accommodation: Flight crew of two on flight deck and various arrangements in main cabin for 8–15 passengers. Optional arrangements for 19 passengers and provision included in basic design for additional emergency exits which will permit up to 34 passengers to be carried.

Status: First prototype flown on 21 September 1984, with second following on 30 August 1985, and certification planned for March 1986.

Notes: The Mystère-Falcon 900 is a derivative of the Mystère-Falcon 50 (see 1982 edition) with which it shares some component commonality, but it features a longer, larger-diameter fuselage, longer span wing and higher-powered engines.

DASSAULT-BREGUET MYSTERE-FALCON 900

Dimensions: Span, 63 ft 5 in (19,33 m); length, 66 ft 5¼ in (20,25 m); height, 24 ft 9¼ in (7,55 m); wing area, 527·77 sq ft (49,03 m²).

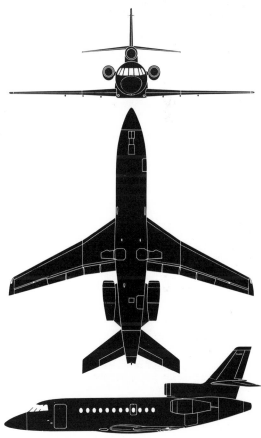

DASSAULT-BREGUET MIRAGE F1

Country of Origin: France.

Type: Single-seat multi-role fighter.

Power Plant: One 11,023 lb st (5 000 kgp) dry and 15,873 lb st (7 200 kgp) reheat SNECMA Atar 9K50 turbojet.

Performance: (F1C) Max speed (clean aircraft), 914 mph (1 470 km/h) or Mach = 1·2 at sea level, 1,450 mph (2 555 km/h) or Mach = 2·2 at 39,370 ft (12 000 m); initial climb, 41,930 ft/min (213 m/sec); service ceiling, 65,600 ft (20 000 m); tactical radius (with two drop tanks and 4,410 lb/ 2 000 kg bombs), 670 mls (1 078 km).

Weights: Empty, 16,314 lb (7 400 kg); normal loaded, 24,030 lb (10 900 kg); max take-off, 32,850 lb (14 900 kg).

Armament: Two 30-mm DEFA 553 cannon and (intercept) one-three Matra 550 Magic plus two AIM-9 AAMs, or (close support) up to 8,818 lb (4 000 kg) of external ordnance.

Status: First of four prototypes flown 23 December 1966, and first production aircraft flown 15 February 1973, with some 665 delivered by beginning of 1986 against orders for 694 and production continuing at a rate of two monthly.

Notes: The last production models for the *Armée de l'Air* consisted of the F1C-200 with fixed flight refuelling probe, the tactical recce F1CR and the two-seat F1B conversion trainer. Whereas the F1C is a dedicated air-air version, the export F1A and F1E are optimised for the air-ground role. The two-seat model retains the Cyrano IV radar, weapon system and missile capability of the F1C, but has no internal guns and fuel capacity is reduced. Foreign orders for the F1 are Ecuador (18), Iraq (113), Jordan (36), Qatar (14), Kuwait (32), Libya (38), Morocco (50), Greece (40), South Africa (48) and Spain (73). The *Armée de l'Air* has received 227 Mirage F1s, comprising 164 F1Cs, 43 F1CRs and 20 F1Bs.

DASSAULT-BREGUET MIRAGE F1

Dimensions: Span, 27 ft 6¾ in (8,40 m); length, 49 ft 2½ in (15,00 m); height, 14 ft 9 in (4,50 m); wing area, 269·1 sq ft (25,00 m²).

DASSAULT-BREGUET MIRAGE 2000

Country of Origin: France.

Type: Single-seat multi-role or (2000N) two-seat low-altitude attack fighter.

Power Plant: One 14,460 lb st (6 560 kgp) dry and 21,385 lb st (9 700 kgp) reheat SNECMA M53-P2 turbofan.

Performance: Max speed (clean), 915 mph or Mach = 1·2 at sea level, 1,550 mph (2 495 km/h) or Mach = 2·35 (short endurance dash) above 36,090 ft (11 000 m); max climb, 49,000 ft/min (249 m/sec); combat radius (intercept mission with two drop tanks and four AAMs), 435 mls (700 km).

Weights: Empty, 16,315 lb (7 400 kg); max take-off, 36,375 lb (16 500 kg).

Armament: Two 30-mm DEFA 554 cannon and (air superiority) two Matra 550 Magic and two Matra Super 530D AAMs, or (close support) up to 13,225 lb (6 000 kg) of external ordnance distributed between nine hardpoints.

Status: First of five prototypes flown 10 March 1978, with 100th aircraft scheduled to fly February–March 1986. By the beginning of 1986, 106 (56 2000Cs, 19 2000Bs and 31 2000Ns) had been funded for the *Armée de l'Air* and export orders comprising 36 for Abu Dhabi, 32 for Egypt, 40 for Greece, 40 for India and 13 for Peru. Production tempo was rising from 3·5 to six aircraft monthly at the beginning of 1986.

Notes: The Mirage 2000 is currently being manufactured in four versions: the 2000C optimised for the air superiority role, the 2000B two-seat trainer, the 2000R single-seat reconnaissance aircraft and the 2000N low-altitude penetration aircraft (see 1985 edition). The last-mentioned version is expected to enter *Armée de l'Air* service in 1988, and will have Antilope V terrain-following and ground-mapping radar, and will be armed with a nuclear missile.

DASSAULT-BREGUET MIRAGE 2000

Dimensions: Span, 29 ft 6 in (9,00 m); length, 47 ft 6⅞ in (14,50 m); wing area, 441·3 sq ft (41,00 m²).

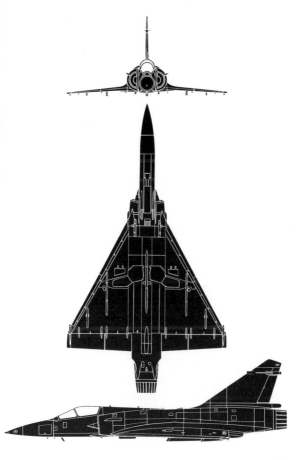

DASSAULT-BREGUET RAFALE

Country of Origin: France.
Type: Single-seat advanced fighter technology demonstrator.
Power Plant: Two 17,000 lb st (7 711 kgp) reheat General Electric F404-GE-100 turbofans.
Performance: (Estimated) Max speed, 1,320 mph (2 124 km/h) plus or Mach = 2·0 plus above 36,000 ft (10 975 m); operational ceiling, 59,000 ft (18 000 m) plus.
Weights: (Estimated) Normal loaded (air defence configuration), 30,860 lb (14 000 kg); max take-off, 44,100 lb (20 000 kg).
Armament: One cannon (probably 30-mm GIAT Mod 791B) and four Matra Mica plus two Matra Magic II missiles for the air defence task. Twelve external stores hardpoints (six under wing and six under fuselage) for loads of up to 7,700 lb (3 500 kg) for the attack mission.
Status: Single prototype of Rafale scheduled to enter flight test in May 1986.
Notes: The primary purpose of the Rafale is, like that of the British Aerospace EAP (see pages 54–55), to test the new technologies that will be embodied in the next generation of combat aircraft, and it is expected to provide a basis for a multi-role combat aircraft required by both the *Armée de l'Air* and the *Aéronavale* in the 'nineties. The Rafale has been designed to afford very high manoeuvrability, a high angle-of-attack capability in combat conditions and good low-speed performance for comparatively short take-off and landing. Considerable use is made of advanced technology materials, most of the wing and some 50 per cent of the fuselage being manufactured from carbon fibre, Allithium replacing conventional light alloys in several parts of the fuselage.

DASSAULT-BREGUET RAFALE

Dimensions: Span, 36 ft 1 in (11,00 m); length, 51 ft 10 in (15,80 m); wing area, 506 sq ft (47,00 m²).

DASSAULT-BREGUET/DORNIER
ALPHA JET NGEA

Countries of Origin: France and Federal Germany.
Type: Tandem two-seat advanced trainer and light tactical support aircraft.
Power Plant: Two 3,175 lb st (1 440 kgp) SNECMA/Turboméca Larzac 04-C20 turbofans.
Performance: Max speed (clean), 572 mph (920 km/h) or Mach=0·86 at 32,800 ft (10 000 m), 645 mph (1 038 km/h) at sea level; max initial climb, 11,220 ft/min (57 m/sec); service ceiling, 48,000 ft (14 630 m); tactical radius (LO-LO-LO with gun pod, two 137·5 Imp gal/625 l drop tanks and underwing ordnance), 391 mls (630 km), (without drop tanks), 242 mls (390 km), (HI-LO-HI with drop tanks), 668 mls (1 075 km), (without drop tanks), 363 mls (583 km).
Weights: Empty equipped, 7,749 lb (3 515 kg); max take-off, 17,637 lb (8 000 kg).
Armament: (Tactical air support) Max of 5,510 lb (2 500 kg) of ordnance distributed between five stations.
Status: The Alpha Jet NGEA entered flight test in April 1982. Four delivered to Egypt in following year by parent company, and co-production with Egyptian industry continuing at rate of two per month at beginning of 1986 against Egyptian orders for 30 of (MS1) training and 30 of (MS 2) attack versions. Six of MS2 version ordered by Cameroun.
Notes: The Alpha Jet NGEA (*Nouvelle Génération Ecole-Appui*) is an improved attack version of the basic aircraft with a nav/attack system and uprated engines.

DASSAULT-BREGUET/DORNIER ALPHA JET NGEA

Dimensions: Span, 29 ft 11 in (9,11 m); length, 40 ft 3 in (12,29 m); height, 13 ft 9 in (4,19 m); wing area, 188 sq ft (17,50 m²).

DE HAVILLAND CANADA DASH 8

Country of Origin: Canada.

Type: Regional airliner and corporate transport.

Power Plant: Two 2,000 shp Pratt & Whitney Canada PW120 turboprops.

Performance: Max cruise speed, 311 mph (500 km/h) at 15,000 ft (4 570 m), 301 mph (484 km/h) at 25,000 ft (7 620 m); max initial climb, 2,070 ft/min (10,51 m/sec); range (36 passengers and IFR reserves), 691 mls (1 112 km) at max cruise at 25,000 ft (7 620 m); max range (with 4,550-lb/2 064-kg payload and max fuel), 1,493 mls (2 402 km).

Weights: Operational empty, 21,590 lb (9 793 kg); max take-off, 33,000 lb (14 968 kg).

Accommodation: Flight crew of two and standard arrangement for 36 passengers four-abreast with central aisle. Alternate arrangements for 38–39 passengers, mixed passenger-cargo operations and corporate executive transportation.

Status: The first of four pre-production prototypes was flown on 20 June 1983, with two more flown in October and November, and a fourth by beginning of 1984. Certification October 1984, with first customer delivery (to NorOntair) in that month, and orders and options exceeding 100 aircraft by December 1985.

Notes: The Dash 8 is an evolutionary design embodying service-proven features of the Dash 7 (see 1984 edition). The corporate version will feature an extended range capability, additional tankage permitting 2,590 miles (4 167 km) to be flown with a 1,200-lb (544-kg) payload at long-range cruise. Six Dash 8Ms ordered in 1984 by Canada's Department of National Defence, four of these as navigational trainers.

DE HAVILLAND CANADA DASH 8

Dimensions: Span, 85 ft 0 in (25,91 m); length, 73 ft 0 in (22,25 m); height, 25 ft 0 in (7,62 m); wing area, 585 sq ft (54,35 m²).

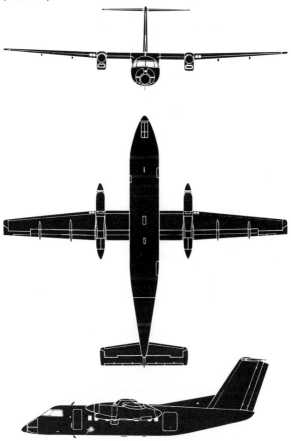

DORNIER DO 228

Country of Origin: Federal Germany.

Type: Light regional airliner and utility transport.

Power Plant: Two 715 shp Garrett AiResearch TPE 331-5 turboprops.

Performance: Max cruise speed, 268 mph (432 km/h) at 10,000 ft (3 280 m), 230 mph (370 km/h) at sea level; initial climb, 2,050 ft/min (10,4 m/sec); service ceiling, 29,600 ft (9 020 m); range (-100), 1,224 mls (1 970 km) at max range cruise, 1,075 mls (1 730 km) at max cruise, (-200), 715 mls (1 150 km) at max range cruise, 640 mls (1 030 km) at max cruise.

Weights: Operational empty (-100), 7,132 lb (3 235 kg), (-200), 7,450 lb (3 379 kg); max take-off, 12,570 lb (5 700 kg).

Accommodation: Flight crew of two and standard arrangements for (-100) 15 and (-200) 19 passengers in individual seats with central aisle.

Status: Prototype Do 228-100 flown on 28 March and -200 on 9 May 1981, and first customer delivery (A/S Norving) August 1982. A total of 94 (plus 23 on option) Do 228s (both -100s and -200s) had been ordered by beginning of October 1985, in which year production rose from three to four aircraft monthly.

Notes: The Do 228 mates a new-technology wing of super-critical section with the fuselage cross-section of the Do 128 (see 1982 edition), and two versions differing essentially in fuselage length and range capability are currently in production, the shorter-fuselage Do 228-100 and the longer-fuselage Do 228-200 (illustrated). All-cargo and corporate transport versions of the -100 are being offered. The -101 and -201 versions offer increased take-off weights. The Do 228 has been selected by India to meet that country's LTA (Light Transport Aircraft) requirement. Ten have been supplied by Dornier with approximately 140 to be built in India by HAL.

DORNIER DO 228

Dimensions: Span, 55 ft 7 in (16,97 m); length (-100) 49 ft 3 in (15,03 m), (-200), 54 ft 3 in (16,55 m); height, 15 ft 9 in (4,86 m); wing area, 344·46 sq ft (32,00 m²).

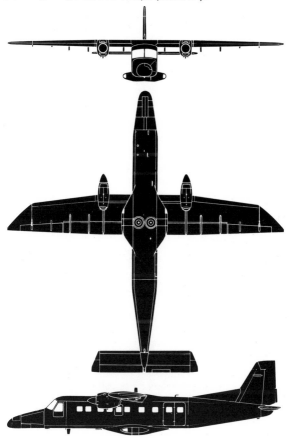

EMBRAER EMB-120 BRASILIA

Country of Origin: Brazil.

Type: Short-haul regional and corporate transport.

Power Plant: Two 1,500 shp Pratt & Whitney (Canada) PW115 turboprops.

Performance: (At 25,350 lb/11 500 kg) Max speed, 359 mph (578 km/h) at 20,000 ft (6 100 m); max cruise, 345 mph (555 km/h) at 20,000 ft (6 100 m); long-range cruise, 303 mph (487 km/h); max initial climb, 2,320 ft/min (11,78 m/sec); range (with 30 passengers and reserves), 691 mls (1 112 km); max range (max fuel and 14 passengers), 1,957 mls (3 150 km).

Weights: Empty equipped (standard), 16,670 lb (7 560 kg); max take-off, 25,350 lb (11 500 kg).

Accommodation: Flight crew of two and optional arrangements for 24, 26 and 30 passengers three abreast with offset aisle.

Status: First, second and third prototypes flown on 27 July and 21 December 1983, and 9 May 1984 respectively, with first customer delivery (to Atlantic Southeast Airlines) following in August 1985. By the beginning of December 1985, orders had been placed for 59 Brasilias and options taken on a further 90 aircraft, with five delivered by the end of 1985, 20 scheduled to be manufactured during 1986, and 25 annually thereafter.

Notes: The first corporate executive version of the Brasilia (in 18-seat configuration) is scheduled to be delivered in 1986 (to United Technologies), in the second half of which year the first deliveries will be made to the Brazilian Air Force (against an initial order for two plus two on option). Maritime surveillance and airborne early warning versions are under development for service with the Brazilian Air Force from the early 'nineties.

EMBRAER EMB-120 BRASILIA

Dimensions: Span, 64 ft 10¾ in (19,78 m); length, 65 ft 7 in (20,00 m); height, 20 ft 10 in (6,35 m); wing area, 424·42 sq ft (39,43 m²).

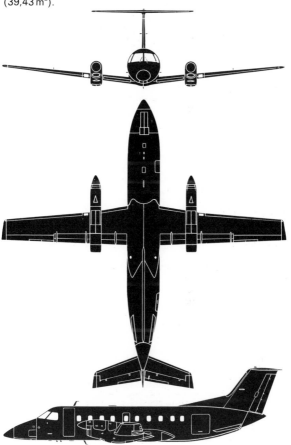

EMBRAER EMB-312 TUCANO

Country of Origin: Brazil.
Type: Tandem two-seat basic trainer.
Power Plant: One 750 shp Pratt & Whitney Canada PT6A-25C turboprop.
Performance: (At 5,622 lb/2 550 kg) Max speed, 269 mph (433 km/h) at 10,000 ft (3 050 m); max cruise, 255 mph (411 km/h) at 10,000 ft (3 050 m); econ cruise, 198 mph (319 km/h); max initial climb, 2,180 ft/min (11,07 m/sec); max range (internal fuel with 30 min reserves), 1,145 mls (1 844 km); ferry range (two 145 Imp gal/660 l external tanks), 2,069 mls (3 330 km).
Weights: Basic empty, 3,991 lb (1 810 kg); loaded (clean), 5,622 lb (2 550 kg); max take-off, 7,000 lb (3 175 kg).
Armament: (Weapons instruction and light strike) External ordnance load of 2,205 lb (1 000 kg) distributed between four wing hardpoints.
Status: First of four prototypes flown on 15 August 1980, with production deliveries to Brazilian Air Force (against order for 118 plus option on further 50) commencing 29 September 1983, with 100th delivered August 1985. Eight delivered to Honduras and 110 (with options on further 60) being assembled at Helwan, Egypt, for the Egyptian and Iraqi (80 plus 20 on option) air forces after delivery of 10 in flyaway condition by Embraer. Production tempo of six monthly (including kits for Egypt).
Notes: A more powerful version of the Tucano was selected in 1985 as the new basic trainer for the RAF. To be manufactured under licence by Shorts, this will be powered by a 1,100 shp Garrett TPE331-12B engine and deliveries against a contract for 130 aircraft will commence before the end of 1986.

EMBRAER EMB-312 TUCANO

Dimensions: Span, 36 ft 6½ in (11,14 m); length, 32 ft 4¼ in (9,86 m); height, 11 ft 1⅞ in (3,40 m); wing area, 208·82 sq ft (19,40 m²).

ENAER T-35 PILLAN

Country of Origin: Chile.

Type: Tandem two-seat primary/basic trainer.

Power Plant: One 300 hp Avco Lycoming AEIO-540-K1K5 six-cylinder horizontally-opposed engine.

Performance: (At max take-off weight) Max speed, 193 mph (311 km/h) at sea level; cruise (75% power), 185 mph (298 km/h) at 8,000 ft (2680 m); max initial climb, 1,516 ft/min (7,7 m/sec); service ceiling, 19,100 ft (5820 m); range (at 75% power with 45 min reserves), 679 mls (1093 km).

Weights: Empty, 1,836 lb (832 kg); empty equipped, 2,048 lb (929 kg); max take-off, 2,900 lb (1315 kg).

Armament: (Training and light attack) Two pods of four or seven rockets, 250-lb (11,4-kg) bombs or 12,7-mm machine gun pods.

Status: First of two prototypes assembled by Piper (PA-28R-300) flown on 6 March 1981. Six pre-series aircraft assembled in Chile and first production aircraft flown on 28 December 1984, with first deliveries to Chilean Air Force on 31 July 1985 against requirement for 80 aircraft. Forty ordered by Spanish Air Force as the Tamiz (Grader).

Notes: The Pillán (Devil) was designed under contract by Piper and embodies some standard components from the PA-28, PA-31 and PA-32 series light aircraft. Manufacture has been progressively transferred to ENAER which will eventually be responsible for some 80 per cent of the airframe content. Two versions are being built for the Chilean Air Force, 60 being to T-35A standard with a simple avionics kit for basic training and 20 having avionics for IFR instruction as T-35Bs.

ENAER T-35 PILLAN

Dimensions: Span, 28 ft 11 in (8,81 m); length, 26 ft 1 in (7,97 m); height, 7 ft $8\frac{1}{8}$ in (7,70 m); wing area, 147 sq ft (13,64 m^2).

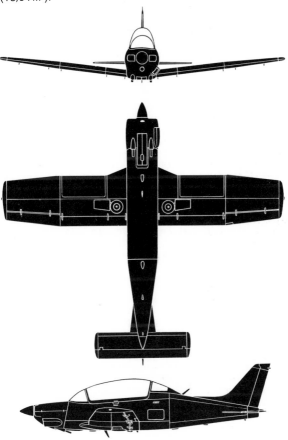

FAIRCHILD T-46A

Country of Origin: USA.

Type: Side-by side two-seat primary/basic trainer.

Power Plant: Two 1,330 lb st (603 kgp) Garrett F109-GA-100 (TFE76-4A) turbofans.

Performance: (Estimated) Max speed, 457 mph (736 km/h) at 25,000 ft (7 620 m); max cruise, 442 mph (712 km/h) at 35,000 ft (10 670 m); econ cruise, 383 mph (616 km/h) at 45,000 ft (13 720 m); max initial climb, 4,470 ft/min (22,7 m/sec); service ceiling, 46,500 ft (14 175 m); ferry range, 1,324 mls (2 130 km).

Weights: Empty, 5,184 lb (2 351 kg); max take-off, 6,817 lb (3 092 kg).

Status: First prototype flown 15 October 1985, with second prototype expected to join the flight test programme April-May 1986. Although some uncertainty attended the future of the T-46A at the time of closing for press, USAF planning called for 650 aircraft through 1992.

Notes: The T-46A was evolved as a successor to the Cessna T-37 in the USAF training syllabus, winning a new-generation trainer contest on 2 July 1982. During the course of 1985, however, the T-46A suffered a number of delays and some cost escalation, and, late year, the USAF was evaluating various alternatives with a view to the possible cancellation of the Fairchild trainer. The T-46A has meanwhile commenced a 22-month flight test programme. Fairchild had earlier proposed an armed export version as the AT-46A, this private venture derivative being considered suitable for armament training, forward air control and light attack duties. This featured four wing hardpoints, the inboard positions being plumbed for 56 Imp gal (254 l) drop tanks with which two 250-lb (113,4-kg) bombs or gun pods could be carried.

FAIRCHILD T-46A

Dimensions: Span, 38 ft 7¾ in (11,78 m); length, 29 ft 6 in (8,99 m); height, 12 ft 8 in (3,86 m); wing area, 160·9 sq ft (14,95 m²).

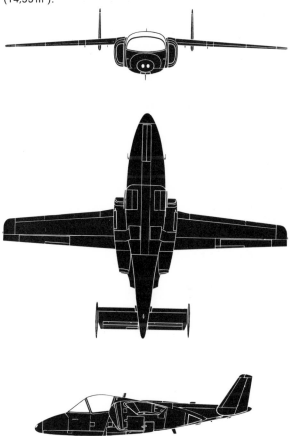

FMA IA 63 PAMPA

Country of Origin: Argentina.
Type: Tandem two-seat basic/advanced trainer.
Power Plant: One 3,500 lb st (1 588 kgp) Garrett TFE731-2N turbofan.
Performance: Max speed (at 7,055 lb/3 200 kg), 460 mph (740 km/h) or Mach = 0·6 at sea level; max initial climb, 5,315 ft/min (27 m/sec); service ceiling, 42,325 ft (12 900 m); range (clean), 930 mls (1 500 km) at 345 mph (560 km/h) at 13,125 ft (4 000 m); tactical radius (attack role with six Mk 81 bombs and 30-mm cannon pod), 224 mls (360 km) HI-LO-HI with 5 min over target and 30 min reserves.
Weights: Normal loaded, 8,156 lb (3 700 kg); max take-off, 11,022 lb (5 000 kg).
Armament: (Training or light attack) One 30-mm cannon pod on fuselage centreline and up to 2,557 lb (1 160 kg) of ordnance distributed between four wing hardpoints.
Status: First and second of three prototypes flown on 6 October 1984 and 7 August 1985 respectively, scheduled to be joined by remaining prototype early 1986. Current planning calls for initial batch of 12 aircraft built against a requirement for 64 aircraft commencing operations at the *Escuela de Aviación Militar* in 1988.
Notes: The Pampa has been developed by Dornier of Federal Germany which now acts only in an advisory capacity to the Fabrica Militar de Aviones (FMA). A version optimised for the light strike role and powered by a 4,300 lb st (1950 kgp) TFE731-5 engine is currently proposed.

FMA IA 63 PAMPA

Dimensions: Span, 31 ft 9½ in (9,69 m); length, 35 ft 10¼ in (10,93 m); height, 14 ft 0¾ in (4,29 m); wing area, 168·24 sq ft (15,63 m^{12}).

FOKKER 50

Country of Origin: Netherlands.

Type: Regional commercial transport.

Power Plant: Two 2,150 shp (2,400 shp emergency) Pratt & Whitney Canada PW124 turboprops.

Performance: (Estimated) Max cruising speed, 332 mph (535 km/h) at 20,000 ft (6 095 m); long-range cruise, 262 mph (421 km/h) at 25,000 ft (7 620 m); max operating altitude, 25,000 ft (7 620 m); range with 50 passengers (at 41,865 lb/18 990 kg), 794 mls (1 278 km), (at 45,900 lb/20 820 kg), 1,808 mls (2 910 km).

Weights: Typical operational empty, 27,300 lb (12 383 kg); max take-off (standard), 41,865 lb (18 990 kg), (optional), 45,900 lb (20 820 kg).

Accommodation: Flight crew of two and standard arrangement for 50 passengers four abreast, with optional layouts for 58–60 passengers in high-density arrangement, or 46 business-class passengers.

Status: First of two prototypes (utilising modified F27 fuselages) was scheduled to enter flight test late December 1985, with second following early 1986. First customer deliveries (to Ansett) in December 1986, with production tempo to peak at two aircraft monthly. Orders for 38 aircraft (plus 12 options) from six customers at beginning of December 1985.

Notes: The Fokker 50 is based on the F27-500 (see 1982 edition) and is unchanged in basic configuration, but in excess of 80 per cent of the component parts are changed or modified, new-technology engines have been adopted, and extensive use is made of composites in the structure.

FOKKER 50

Dimensions: Span, 95 ft 1¾ in (29,00 m); length, 82 ft 7¾ in (25,19 m); height, 28 ft 2½ in (8,60 m); wing area, 753·5 sq ft (70,00 m²).

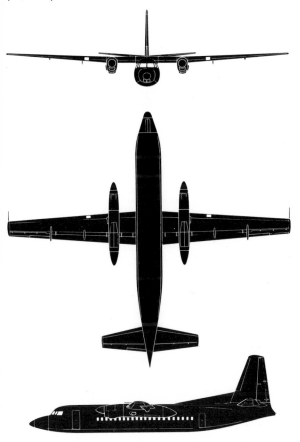

FOKKER 100

Country of Origin: Netherlands.

Type: Short/medium-haul commercial transport.

Power Plant: Two 13,320 lb st (6 042 kgp) Rolls-Royce RB183–03 Tay Mk 620-15 turbofans.

Performance: Max cruising speed, 497 mph (800 km/h) at 35,000 ft (10 670 m) or Mach=0·75; econ cruise, 475 mph (765 km/h) or Mach=0·72; range (at 92,000-lb/41 730-kg MTOW with 107 passengers) at econ cruise, 1,330 mls (2 140 km), (at optional 95,000-lb/43 092-kg MTOW), 1,698 mls (2 733 km).

Weights: Operational empty, 51,260 lb (23 251 kg); standard max take-off, 92,000 lb (41 730 kg); optional max take-off, 95,000 lb (43 092 kg).

Accommodation: Flight crew of two and standard seating for 107 passengers five abreast, optional arrangements including 60 business class and 45 economy class seats, or 12 first class and 80–85 economy class seats.

Status: Two prototypes scheduled to enter flight test during second quarter of 1986, with certification following early 1987. First customer delivery (to Swissair) spring 1987, and anticipated production tempo of three monthly. Thirty-eight aircraft had been ordered by December 1985, with a further 31 on option.

Notes: The Fokker 100 is technically a derivative of the F28 (see 1985 edition), but makes extensive use of technology developed from the abortive F29 and MDF-100. Apart from new engines, the Fokker 100 has new systems and equipment, a lenthened fuselage, and aerodynamically redesigned and extended wings.

FOKKER 100

Dimensions: Span, 92 ft 1½ in (28,08 m); length, 115 ft 10 in (35,31 m); height, 27 ft 10½ in (8,60 m); wing area, 977·4 sq ft (90,80 m²).

GATES LEARJET 55

Country of Origin: USA.

Type: Light corporate executive transport.

Power Plant: Two 3,700 lb st (1 678 kgp) Garrett TFE 731-3A-2B turbofans.

Performance: Max speed, 549 mph (884 km/h) at 30,000 ft (9 150 m); max cruise, 524 mph (843 km/h) at 41,000 ft (12 500 m); econ cruise, 482 mph (776 km/h) at 47,000 ft (14 325 m); max initial climb, 4,560 ft/min (23,16 m/sec); range (with two crew and four passengers with 45 min reserves), 2,642 mls (4 252 km).

Weights: Empty, 12,130 lb (5 502 kg); max take-off, 21,500 lb (9 752 kg).

Accommodation: Flight crew of two and seating for four to eight passengers in differing interior layouts in main cabin.

Status: First of two prototypes flown on 19 April 1979, with first production aircraft following on 11 August 1980. Customer deliveries commenced 30 April 1981, with the 100th aircraft being delivered by 1 June 1984. Production was suspended in September 1984, but resumed mid 1985 at a rate of 0·75 aircraft monthly.

Notes: Originally known as the Longhorn, the Learjet 55 is available in basic form (described above) and in 55ER extended-range and 55LR long-range versions. These have an additional fuel tank in the tailcone baggage compartment (available for refit to basic 55s), and the 55LR has, in addition, a further tank between the standard fuselage tank and the rear cabin baggage compartment.

GATES LEARJET 55

Dimensions: Span, 43 ft 9½ in (13,34 m); length, 55 ft 1½ in (16,79 m); height, 14 ft 8 in (4,47 m); wing area, 264·5 sq ft (24,57 m²).

GATES-PIAGGIO GP-180 AVANTI

Countries of Origin: Italy and USA.
Type: Light corporate transport.
Power Plant: Two 800 shp Pratt & Whitney Canada PT6A-66 turboprops.
Performance: (Estimated) Max speed, 460 mph (740 km/h) at 27,000 ft (8 230 m); econ cruise, 368 mph (593 km/h) at 41,000 ft (12 500 m); max initial climb, 3,650 ft/min (18,54 m/sec); max ceiling, 41,000 ft (12 495 m); range (with four passengers and NBAA reserves), 2,415 mls (3 887 km) at econ cruise.
Weights: Empty equipped, 6,200 lb (2 812 kg); max take-off, 9,800 lb (4 445 kg).
Accommodation: Pilot and co-pilot/passenger on flight deck with standard executive main cabin configuration for seven passengers in individual seats.
Status: First prototype scheduled to fly (in Italy) in March or April 1986, with the second and third joining the flight test programme (in Italy and the USA respectively) in the following summer and autumn. First deliveries anticipated late 1987.
Notes: The Avanti is being developed by Rinaldo Piaggio in Italy and Gates Learjet in the USA, the latter being responsible for the design, development and manufacture of the cockpit and cabin section. Both partners are to establish final assembly lines. The Avanti is of so-called "three-surface" concept, the foreplane balancing the aft located mainplain, a tailplane being retained for pitch control. This arrangement is claimed to result in significant aerodynamic benefits.

GATES-PIAGGIO GP-180 AVANTI

Dimensions: Span, 45 ft 4⅛ in (13,84 m); length, 46 ft 5⅞ in (14,17 m); height, 12 ft 9½ in (3,90 m); wing area, 169·86 sq ft (15,78 m²).

GENERAL DYNAMICS F-16 FIGHTING FALCON

Country of Origin: USA.

Type: (F-16C) Single-seat multi-role fighter and (F-16D) two-seat operational trainer.

Power Plant: One 14,800 lb st (6 713 kgp) dry and 23,830 lb st (10 809 kgp) reheat Pratt & Whitney F100-PW-200 or -220, or 16,610 lb st (7 334 kgp) dry and 27,080 lb st (12 283 kgp) reheat General Electric F110-GE-100 turbofan.

Performance: (F-16C with F100-PW-200) Max speed (short endurance dash), 1,333 mph (2 145 km/h) at 40,000 ft (12 190 m) or Mach=2·02, (sustained), 1,247 mph (2 007 km/h) or Mach=1·89; tactical radius (HI-LO-HI interdiction on internal fuel), 360 mls (580 km) with six 500-lb (227-kg) bombs.

Weights: (F-16C) Take-off (intercept mission with AAMs), 25,070 lb (11 372 kg); max take-off, 37,500 lb (17 010 kg).

Armament: One 20-mm M61A-1 rotary cannon and (intercept) two to six AIM-9L/M AAMs, or (interdiction) up to 12,430 lb (5 638 kg) ordnance distributed between nine stations (with full internal fuel).

Status: First of two (YF-16) prototypes flown 20 January 1974, and first production aircraft (F-16A) flown 7 August 1978, with first F-16C being delivered 19 July 1984. The 1,000th F-16 assembled by parent company delivered to USAF in June 1985. European multination programme embraces 160 for Belgium, 70 for Denmark, 72 for Norway and 213 for Netherlands. Other purchasers include Egypt (80), Greece (40), Israel (150), South Korea (36), Pakistan (40), Turkey (160) and Venezuela (24). Upgraded F-16C and D have common engine bay for either F100 or F110 from 1986.

Notes: The F-16C and F-16D aircraft ordered by Turkey are to be licence-manufactured in that country with deliveries commencing in 1988.

GENERAL DYNAMICS F-16 FIGHTING FALCON

Dimensions: Span (excluding missiles), 31 ft 0 in (9,45 m); length, 47 ft 7¾ in (14,52 m); height, 16 ft 5¼ in (5,01 m); wing area, 300 sq ft (27,87 m²).

GRUMMAN E-2C HAWKEYE

Country of Origin: USA.

Type: Airborne early warning, surface surveillance and strike control aircraft.

Power Plant: Two 4,910 ehp Allison T56-A-425 turboprops.

Performance: Max speed, 348 mph (560 km/h) at 10,000 ft (3 050 m); max range cruise, 309 mph (498 km/h); initial climb, 2,515 ft/min (12,8 m/sec); service ceiling, 30,800 ft (9 390 m); mission endurance (at 230 mls/370 km from base), 4·0 hrs; max endurance, 6·1 hrs; ferry range, 1,604 mls (2 580 km).

Weights: Empty, 38,009 lb (17 240 kg); max take-off, 51,900 lb (23 540 kg).

Accommodation: Crew of five comprising flight crew of two and Airborne Tactical Data System team of three, each occupying an independent operating station.

Status: First of two E-2C prototypes flown on 20 January 1971, with first production aircraft flying on 23 September 1972. Some 90 of 103 ordered by US Navy delivered by beginning of 1986, when planned production was scheduled to continue at a rate of six annually into the early 'nineties. Four delivered to Israel, and first four of eight ordered by Japan delivered in 1983. First of four E-2Cs for Egypt (the 100th production E-2C) delivered 3 October 1985.

Notes: The E-2C is the current production version of the Hawkeye, having followed 59 E-2As (all subsequently up-dated to E-2B standards), and is able to operate independently, in co-operation with other aircraft, or in concert with a ground environment. Two have been delivered to the US Navy as TE-2Cs for use as conversion trainers by the Service's two Hawkeye readiness squadrons which support 12 four-aircraft Hawkeye squadrons attached to the carrier air wings. The E-2X is a proposed simplified export version of the Hawkeye.

GRUMMAN E-2C HAWKEYE

Dimensions: Span, 80 ft 7 in (24,56 m); length, 57 ft 7 in (17,55 m); height, 18 ft 4 in (5,69 m); wing area, 700 sq ft (65,03 m²).

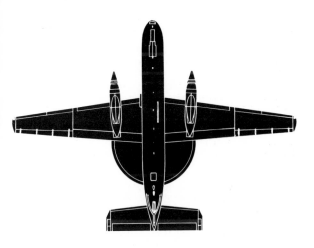

GRUMMAN F-14A (PLUS) TOMCAT

Country of Origin: USA.

Type: Two-seat shipboard multi-role fighter.

Power Plant: Two 16,610 lb st (7 334 kgp) dry and 27,080 lb st (12 283 kgp) reheat General Electric F110-GE-400 turbofans.

Performance: Max speed (with four semi-recessed Sparrow AAMs), 912 mph (1 468 km/h) at sea level or Mach=1·2, 1,544 mph (2 485 km/h) at 40,000 ft or Mach=2·34; combat air patrol loiter time (at 173-mile/278-km radius with two 280 US gal/1060 l drop tanks), 2·05 hrs; combat air patrol radius (with 1 hr loiter), 423 mls (680 km); intercept radius (at Mach=1·3), 319 mls (513 km).

Weights: (Estimated) Empty, 42,000 lb (19 050 kg); max take-off, 75,000 lb (34 020 kg).

Armament: One 20-mm M61A-1 rotary cannon and (typical) four AIM-54A Phoenix, two AIM-7E/F Sparrow and two AIM-9G/H Sidewinder air-to-air missiles.

Status: First production F-14A (Plus) scheduled to enter flight test in August 1986, and further 28 will be delivered (to complete procurement of 599 F-14As) before commencement of delivery of 300 similarly-powered F-14Ds of which first to be received by US Navy in March 1990.

Notes: The F-14A (Plus) version of the Tomcat differs from the basic F-14A essentially in having F110 engines in place of Pratt & Whitney TF30-P-414A which afford some 30 per cent less power. Deliveries of the F-14A (Plus) will commence in April 1988, and it is expected that a number of existing TF30-engined F-14As will be cycled through a re-engining programme. The F-14D will have similar F110 engines and upgraded avionics, including a new digital radar and much improved electronic countermeasures capability.

GRUMMAN F-14A (PLUS) TOMCAT

Dimensions: Span (20 deg sweep), 64 ft 1½ in (19,55 m), (68 deg sweep), 37 ft 7 in (11,45 m); length, 61 ft 11⅞ in (18,90 m); height, 16 ft 0 in (4,88 m); wing area, 565 sq ft (52,50 m²).

GULFSTREAM AEROSPACE GULFSTREAM IV

Country of Origin: USA.

Type: Corporate transport.

Power Plant: Two 12,420 lb st (5 634 kgp) Rolls-Royce Tay Mk 610-8 turbofans.

Performance: Max cruising speed, 577 mph (928 km/h) at 35,000 ft (10 670 m) or Mach = 0·85; long-range cruise, 529 mph (851 km/h) or Mach = 0·8; max initial climb, 4,350 ft/min (22 m/sec); service ceiling, 45,000 ft (13 715 m); max range (at Mach = 0·8 with eight passengers and 45 min reserves), 5,222 mls (8 404 km), (at Mach = 0.85), 4,053 mls (6 523 km).

Weights: Manufacturer's empty, 33,400 lb (15 150 kg); operational empty (typical), 39,300 lb (17 826 kg); max take-off, 69,700 lb (31 615 kg).

Accommodation: Flight crew of two and standard cabin arrangement for 14 passengers with optional arrangements for up to 19 passengers.

Status: Prototype flown for first time on 19 September 1985, with certification and initial customer deliveries scheduled for mid 1986. More than 80 Gulfstream IVs ordered by beginning of 1986, and production tempo to attain four monthly by 1987.

Notes: Essentially a progressive development of the Gulfstream III (see 1984 edition), the Gulfstream IV features a structurally redesigned wing, a lengthened fuselage and Tay engines in place of Speys. An airliner version with an 18·5 ft (5,64 m) fuselage stretch, the Gulfstream IVB, is proposed, offering accommodation for 24 first-class passengers over a range of 4,605 mls (7 410 km), and a military surveillance reconnaissance aircraft (SRA) version was under consideration at the beginning of 1986.

GULFSTREAM AEROSPACE GULFSTREAM IV

Dimensions: Span, 77 ft 10 in (23,72 m); length, 87 ft 7 in (26,70 m); height, 24 ft 4 in (7,42 m); wing area, 950·39 sq ft (88,29 m²).

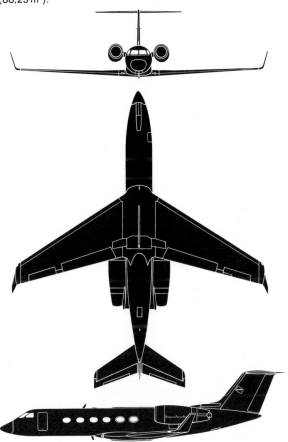

HARBIN YUN-12 TURBO-PANDA

Country of Origin: China.

Type: Light STOL general-purpose transport.

Power Plant: Two (Yun-12-I) 500 shp Pratt & Whitney Canada PT6A-11 or (Yun-12-II) 620 shp PT6A-27 turbo-props.

Performance: (Yun-12-II) Max speed, 187 mph (302 km/h) at 9,840 ft (3 000 m); cruise, 149 mph (240 km/h) at 9,840 ft (3 000 m); max initial climb, 1,575 ft/min (8,0 m/sec); range (17 passengers and baggage), 255 mls (410 km) with 45 min reserves.

Weights: Operational empty, 6,614 lb (3 000 kg); max take-off, 12,125 lb (5 500 kg).

Accommodation: Crew of two on flight deck with three abreast seating in main cabin for up to 17 passengers. Alternative arrangements for aeromedical and all-cargo versions.

Status: The first of three Yun-12-I prototypes was flown on 14 July 1982, the series version being the Yun-12-II.

Notes: The Yun-12, which is being offered for export as the Turbo-Panda, is a progressive development of the piston-engined seven-passenger Yun-11. Whereas the Yun-12-I was essentially a re-engined version of the earlier type, the Yun-12-II has a lengthened fuselage of increased cross section, a new aerofoil section and increased fuel capacity. The Hong Kong Aircraft Engineering Company (HAECO) has designed a new cabin interior and environmental control system for the Yun-12, and drawings and kits are being provided for use in Yun-12s on the assembly line or already delivered. The Yun-12 is one of the first aircraft of *entirely* Chinese indigenous design to attain production status.

HARBIN YUN-12 TURBO-PANDA

Dimensions: Span, 56 ft 10½ in (17,23 m); length, 48 ft 9 in (14,86 m); height, 17 ft 3¾ in (5,27 m); wing area, 368·88 sq ft (34,27 m²).

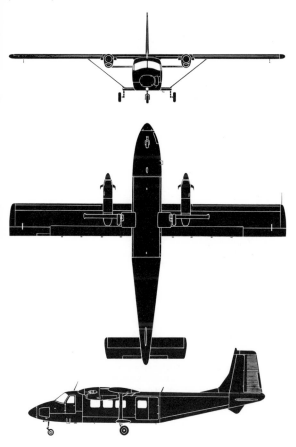

HAWKER DE HAVILLAND A 10B

Country of Origin: Australia.
Type: Side-by-side two-seat trainer.
Power Plant: One 550 shp Pratt & Whitney Canada PT6A-25D turboprop.
Performance: (Estimated) Max speed, 234 mph (376 km/h) at 15,000 ft (4 570 m); max cruise, 207 mph (333 km/h) at sea level; max initial climb, 1,840 ft/min (9,35 m/sec); time to 10,000 ft (3 050 m), 5·5 min; endurance (with 50 min reserves), 3 hrs.
Weights: Empty equipped, 3,073 lb (1 394 kg); loaded (normal training mission), 4,409 lb (2 000 kg); max take-off (utility), 5,732 lb (2 600 kg).
Status: First of two prototypes was scheduled for roll-out on 1 December 1985, with flight testing to commence mid-1986. RAAF requirement for 69 aircraft, but owing to development delays and cost overruns, the production future of the A 10 was in some doubt at the time of closing for press.
Notes: Designed to meet the requirements of an RAAF specification, the A 10 was originally being developed by the Australian Aircraft Consortium (AAC) formed by Commonwealth Aircraft, Hawker de Havilland and the Government Aircraft Factories. With the absorption of Commonwealth by Hawker de Havilland in 1985, the latter took over the responsibility for the A 10 programme, the Government Aircraft Factories effectively becoming sub-contractors. By late 1985, when the A 10 was competing with a licence-built Pilatus PC-7 for the RAAF order, Hawker de Havilland had submitted proposals for design simplification as the A 10B and alternative engines, including the Garrett TPE331-10H.

HAWKER DE HAVILLAND A 10B

Dimensions: Span, 36 ft 1 in (11,00 m); length, 32 ft 10 in (10,01 m); height, 12 ft 1⅔ in (3,70 m); wing area, 215·3 sq ft (20,00 m²).

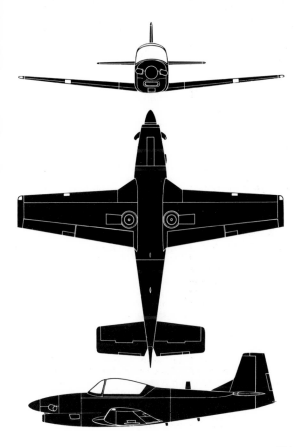

IAI LAVI

Country of Origin: Israel.

Type: Single-seat multirole fighter and two-seat conversion trainer.

Power Plant: One 13,550 lb st (6 146 kgp) military and 20,600 lb st (9 344 kgp) reheat Pratt & Whitney PW1120 turbojet.

Performance: (Estimated) Max speed (two IR missiles and half fuel), 1,220 mph (1 963 km/h) at 40,000 ft (12 190 m) or Mach = 1·85; low-altitude penetration speed (two IR missiles and eight 750-lb/340-kg bombs), 620 mph (998 km/h), two IR missiles and two 2,000-lb/907-kg bombs), 687 mph (1 106 km/h); combat radius LO-LO-LO (two IR missiles and eight 750-lb/340-kg bombs), 280 mls (450 km), HI-LO-HI (two IR missiles and two 2,000-lb/907-kg bombs), 1,150+ mls (1 850+ km).

Weights: (Estimated) Max take-off, 42,500 lb (19 278 kg).

Armament: Max of 20,000 lb (9 072 kg) external ordnance on four underwing, four underfuselage and two wingtip stations.

Status: First of four single-seat and two two-seat prototypes scheduled to enter flight test during September 1986, with first production deliveries commencing 1990. Israeli requirement for 300 aircraft, including 60 combat-capable two-seaters, with IOC (Initial Operational Capability) scheduled for 1992.

Notes: The Lavi (young Lion) is intended for close air support and interdiction with a secondary air-air role. Twenty-two per cent of structure weight comprises composite materials, Grumman having been responsible for wing and fin design and development. The combat-capable two-seat version is illustrated by the three-view drawing opposite.

IAI LAVI

Dimensions: Span, 28 ft 7 in (8,71 m); Length, 47 ft 2½ in (14,39 m); height, 17 ft 4 in (5,28 m); wing area, 349·8 sq ft (32,50 m²).

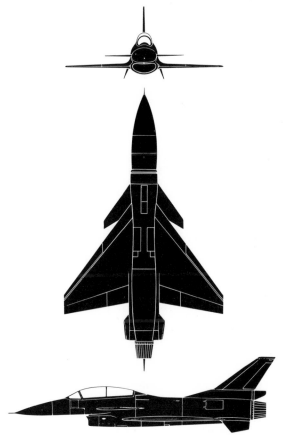

IAI WESTWIND ASTRA

Country of Origin: Israel.

Type: Light corporate transport.

Power Plant: Two 3,700 lb st (1 678 kgp) Garrett TFE371-3B-200G turbofans.

Performance: Max cruising speed (at 16,000 lb/7 258 kg), 535 mph (862 km/h) at 35,000 ft (10 670 m) or Mach = 0·8; long-range cruise, 462 mph (743 km/h) or Mach = 0·7; max initial climb (at max take-off weight), 3,560 ft/min (18,08 m/sec); ceiling, 45,000 ft (13 715 m); range at long-range cruise (two crew and four passengers), 3,454 mls (5 560 km) with 45 min reserves; max fuel range, 3,685 mls (5 930 km); max payload range, 2,648 mls (4 262 km).

Weights: Basic operational (typical including crew), 12,790 lb (5 801 kg); max take-off, 23,500 lb (10 660 kg).

Accommodation: Flight crew of two and standard accommodation for six passengers with rear cabin seats convertible as sleeperettes. Two- and three-place divans optional to increase capacity to max of eight passengers.

Status: First and second prototypes flown on 19 March and 26 July 1984 respectively. FAA certification obtained on 1 September 1985, with customer deliveries commencing in February 1986. Production rate of one aircraft monthly from early 1986, with ability to increase to three monthly if warranted by orders.

Notes: The Westwind Astra retains the basic fuselage of the earlier Westwind II, together with engine nacelles and horizontal tail, but embodies some stretch and entirely new and repositioned wing offering a considerable improvement in transonic drag.

124

IAI WESTWIND ASTRA

Dimensions: Span, 52 ft 8 in (16,05 m); length, 52 ft 9 in (16,08 m); height, 17 ft $10\frac{3}{4}$ in (5,45 m); wing area, 316·6 sq ft (29,41 m²).

IAv CRAIOVA IAR-99 SOIM

Country of Origin: Romania.

Type: Tandem two-seat advanced trainer and light attack aircraft.

Power Plant: One 4,000 lb st (1 814 kgp) Tubomecanica-built Rolls-Royce Viper Mk 632-41 turbojet.

Performance: Max speed (at 12,072 lb/5 476 kg), 537 mph (865 km/h) at sea level or Mach=0·783, 502 mph (808 km/h) at 30,000 ft (9 145 m); max initial climb, 7,185 ft/min (36,5 m/sec); service ceiling, 45,600 ft (13 900 m).

Weights: Empty equipped, 6,878 lb (3 120 kg); max take-off, 12,072 lb (5 476 kg).

Armament: Four wing hardpoints of 772 lb (350 kg) capacity inboard and 551 lb (250 kg) capacity outboard for rocket packs, gun pods and light bombs, and provision beneath fuselage for one 23-mm GSh-23L twin-barrel cannon pod.

Status: Prototype testing initiated April 1985. No details available of production status at beginning of 1986, but reported that the Romanian Air Force has a requirement for 100–150 aircraft in this category.

Notes: The Soim (Hawk) has been designed and built by the Intreprinderea de Avioane (IAv) at Craiova to meet a requirement for an advanced pilot training aircraft with secondary ground attack capabilities drawn up by the Romanian Air Force in the late 'seventies. The Soim is intended to carry pilots from such piston-engined trainers as the IAR-823 to two-seat conversion training versions of combat aircraft types, such as the MiG-21U and MiG-23U, and the two-seat variant of the IAR-93A attack aircraft.

IAv CRAIOVA IAR-99 SOIM

Dimensions: Span, 32 ft 3¼ in (9,85 m); length, 35 ft 8¼ in (10,88 m); height, 12 ft 9 in (3,89 m); wing area, 201·4 sq ft (18,71 m²).

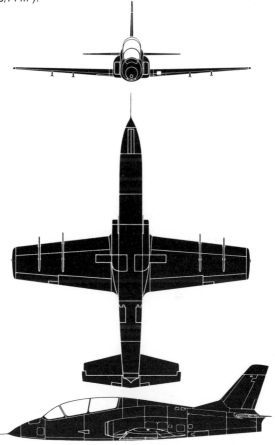

ILYUSHIN IL-76 (CANDID)

Country of Origin: USSR.
Type: Heavy-duty medium/long-haul military and commercial freighter and troop transport.
Power Plant: Four 26,455 lb st (12 000 kgp) Soloviev D-30KP turbofans.
Performance: Max speed, 528 mph (850 km/h) at 32,810 ft (10 000 m); max cruise, 497 mph (800 km/h) at 29,500–42,650 ft (9 000–13 000 m); range cruise, 466 mph (750 km/h); initial climb, 1,772 ft/min (9,0 m/sec); range (with max payload), 1,864 mls (3 000 km) with 45 min reserves, (with 44,032-lb/20 000-kg payload), 4,040 mls (6 500 km).
Weights: Max take-off, 374,790 lb (170 000 kg).
Armament: (Military) Twin 23-mm cannon in tail barbette.
Accommodation: Normal flight crew of seven (including two freight handlers) with navigator's compartment below flight deck in glazed nose. Quick configuration changes may be made by means of modules each of which can accommodate 30 passengers in four abreast seating, litter patients and medical attendants, or cargo. Three such modules may be carried, these being loaded through the rear doors by means of overhead travelling cranes. Wheeled or tracked vehicles, self-propelled anti-aircraft guns, etc, may be loaded over 66,140-lb (30 000-kg) capacity ramp.
Status: First of four prototypes flown on 25 March 1971, with production deliveries to both Aeroflot and the Soviet Air Forces following in 1974. More than 50 in service with former and 250 with latter by beginning of 1986, when production was continuing at approximately 30 annually.
Notes: Since introduction of the basic Il-76, developed versions have included the Il-76T with additional fuel tankage, the military Il-76M (Candid-B), and the improved Il-76TD and MD. An airborne early warning derivative (see 1985 edition) is known to NATO as Mainstay.

ILYUSHIN IL-76 (CANDID)

Dimensions: Span, 165 ft 8⅓ in (50,50 m); length, 152 ft 10¼ in (46,59 m); height, 48 ft 5⅓ in (14,76 m); wing area, 3,229·2 sq ft (300,00 m²).

ILYUSHIN IL-86 (CAMBER)

Country of Origin: USSR.

Type: Medium-haul commercial airliner.

Power Plant: Four 28,660 lb st (13 000 kgp) Kuznetsov NK-86 turbofans.

Performance: Max cruising speed, 590 mph (950 km/h) at 29,530 ft (9 000 m); econ cruise, 559 mph (900 km/h) at 36,090 ft (11 000 m); range (with max payload—350 passengers), 2,485 mls (4 000 km), (with 250 passengers), 3,107 mls (5 000 km).

Weights: Max take-off, 454,150 lb (206 000 kg).

Accommodation: Basic flight crew of three-four and up to 350 passengers nine-abreast with two aisles and divided between three cabins seating 111, 141 and 98 passengers.

Status: First prototype flown on 22 December 1976, and production prototype flown on 24 October 1977. Deliveries to Aeroflot commenced 1980, and some 70–80 are believed to have been delivered by the beginning of 1986. The Polish WSK-Mielec concern is responsible for manufacture of the entire wing, stabiliser and engine pylons. Four Il-86s were originally to have been delivered to Polish Airlines LOT.

Notes: The Il-86 operated its first scheduled service (Moscow–Tashkent) on 26 December 1980, and first international service (Moscow–Prague) on 12 October 1981, but there has been an unexplained slippage in Aeroflot's programmed introduction of the Il-86 on many routes and it is believed that performance has fallen short of expectations. It is anticipated that production will be restricted in favour of the longer-range derivative type, the Il-96, which will be powered by new turbofans in the 35,300 lb st (16 000 kgp) category and a supercritical wing swept 30 deg (as compared with the 35 deg of the Il-86). Max take-off weight will be 507,000 lb (230 000 kg). Sub-assemblies for the Il-96 are to be manufactured by the WSK-Mielec in Poland.

ILYUSHIN IL-86 (CAMBER)

Dimensions: Span, 157 ft 8$\frac{1}{8}$ in (48,06 m); length, 195 ft 4 in (59,54 m); height, 51 ft 10$\frac{1}{2}$ in (15,81 m); wing area, 3,550 sq ft (329,80 m²).

KAWASAKI T-4

Country of Origin: Japan.

Type: Tandem two-seat basic trainer.

Power Plant: Two 3,660 lb st (1 660 kgp) Ishikawajima-Harima XF3-30 turbofans.

Performance: (Estimated) Max speed, 576 mph (927 km/h) at sea level or Mach = 0·75, 616 mph (990 km/h) at 25,000 ft (7 620 m) or Mach = 0·9; max continuous cruise, 506 mph (815 km/h) at 30,000 ft (9 145 m); max initial climb, 10,000 ft/min (50,8 m/sec); service ceiling, 40,000 ft (12 200 m); range (internal fuel), 863 mls (1 390 km).

Weights: Empty, 8,157 lb (3 700 kg); normal loaded, 12,125 lb (5 500 kg); max take-off, 16,535 lb (7 500 kg).

Armament: One 7,6-mm machine gun pod on fuselage hardpoint and one AIM-9L Sidewinder AAM on each of two wing hardpoints.

Status: The first of four prototypes (XT-4s) was flown on 29 July 1985, with remaining three prototypes scheduled to enter test in February, April and June 1986 respectively. Delivery of first production T-4 for the Air Self-Defence Force is scheduled for mid-1988, and current planning calls for procurement of 200-250 aircraft.

Notes: The T-4 has been developed jointly by Kawasaki (as prime contractor), Mitsubishi and Fuji as a successor to the Fuji T-1. Mitsubishi is responsible for the centre and rear fuselage, the engine air intakes and vertical tail, Fuji contributing the wings, horizontal tail surfaces, rear fuselage and cockpit canopy, and Kawasaki producing the front fuselage and undertaking final assembly. The T-4 is the first Japanese aircraft to combine an airframe of indigenous design with a nationally-designed aero engine in 25 years.

KAWASAKI T-4

Dimensions: Span, 32 ft 6 in (9,90 m); length, 42 ft 8 in (13,00 m); height, 15 ft 1 in (4,60 m); wing area, 232·5 (21,60 m²).

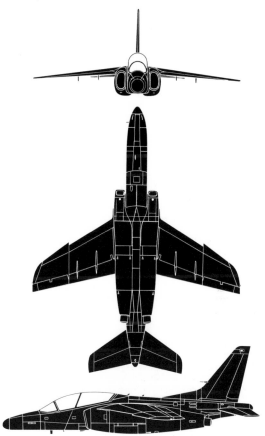

LET L-410UVP-E TURBOLET

Country of Origin: Czechoslovakia.
Type: Light general-purpose transport.
Power Plant: Two 750 shp Walter M 601 E turboprops.
Performance: Max speed, 236 mph (380 km/h) at 13,780 ft (4 200 m); max cruise, 227 mph (365 km/h) at 9,840 ft (3 000 m); econ cruise, 186 mph (300 km/h); range (with max payload and 30 min reserves), 329 mls (530 km).
Weights: Empty, 8,708 lb (3 950 kg); max take-off, 14,110 lb (6 400 kg).
Accommodation: Flight crew of two and up to 19 passengers three abreast with offset aisle.
Status: The first prototype Turbolet (XL-410) was flown on 16 April 1969, and the aircraft has been in continuous production since 1970 in successive versions, with nearly 700 delivered by the beginning of 1986 of which more than 500 have been supplied to the Soviet Union (10 L-410As, 100 L-410Ms and the remainder L-410UVPs). The standard production version since the beginning of 1979 has been the L-410UVP (illustrated above), the first of three prototypes of which first flew on 1 November 1977, and the L-410UVP-E (illustrated on opposite page), which entered flight test early 1985, is scheduled to enter production early in 1986. Current production rate is six-eight monthly.
Notes: The Turbolet is available for both civil and military roles, and in the former serves with the Czech, East German and Libyan air forces among others. The L-410UVP-E differs from the standard UVP in having optional wingtip fuel tanks, five- rather than three-bladed propellers and uprated engines, max take-off weight being increased by 1,320 lb (600 kg). Internally, the new model has been modified to seat four more passengers.

LET L-410UVP-E TURBOLET

Dimensions: Span (over tip tanks), 65 ft 2½ in (19,88 m), (without tip tanks), 63 ft 11 in (19,49 m); length, 47 ft 6 in (14,48 m); height, 19 ft 1½ in (5,83 m); wing area, 378·67 sq ft (35,18 m²).

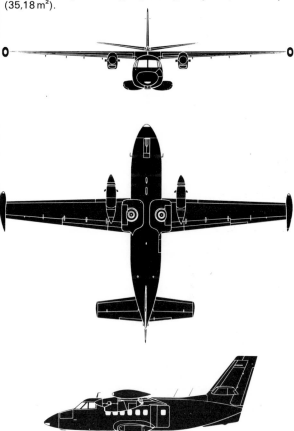

LOCKHEED C-5B GALAXY

Country of Origin: USA.

Type: Heavy strategic transport.

Power Plant: Four 41,100 lb st (18 643 kgp) General Electric TF39-GE-1C turbofans.

Performance: Max speed, 571 mph (919 km/h) at 25,000 ft (7 620 m); max cruise, 552–564 mph (888–908 km/h) at 25,000 ft (7 620 m); econ cruise, 518 mph (833 km/h); max initial climb, 1,725 ft/min (8,75 m/sec); range (with max payload), 2,728 mls (4 390 km), (max fuel and reserves), 6,850 mls (11 024 km).

Weights: Operational empty, 374,000 lb (169 643 kg); max take-off, 769,000 lb (348 820 kg).

Accommodation: Flight crew of five plus 15 seats on flight deck, 75 seats in aft troop compartment and up to 270 troops on pallet-mounted seats in cargo compartment. Up to 36 standard 463L cargo pallets, or various vehicles.

Status: First flight of C-5B took place on 10 September 1985 and first delivery to USAF was planned for December 1985 against requirement for 50 aircraft. Production is to peak in January 1988 at two per month with the 23rd aircraft.

Notes: Production of 81 examples of the C-5A was completed in May 1973, manufacture of the Galaxy being reinstated in 1982 with the C-5B. Although external aerodynamic configuration and internal arrangements remain unchanged between the C-5A and C-5B, the latter differs in respect of some items of equipment and incorporates from the outset various significant improvements already made on or proposed for the rewinged C-5As, all 77 of which will have passed through the rewinging programme by July 1987. Apart from a new wing, the C-5B features engines of increased thrust, state-of-the-art avionics and carbon brakes. The C-5B is claimed to incorporate some 40 improvements over the earlier C-5A.

LOCKHEED C-5B GALAXY

Dimensions: Span, 222 ft 8½ in (67,88 m); length, 247 ft 10 in (75,53 m); height, 65 ft 1½ in (19,34 m); wing area, 6,200 sq ft (575,98 m²).

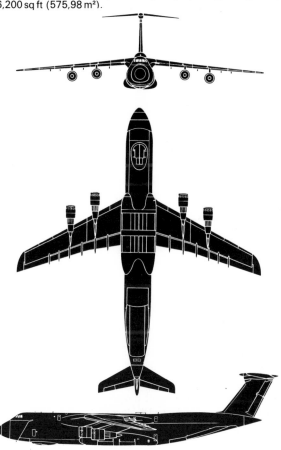

LOCKHEED L-100-30 HERCULES

Country of Origin: USA.

Type: Medium/long-range military and commercial freight transport.

Power Plant: Four 4,508 ehp Allison T56-A-15 turboprops.

Performance: Max cruise speed, 386 mph (620 km/h) at 20,000 ft (6 095 m); long-range cruise, 345 mph (556 km/h); range (max payload), 2,300 mls (3 700 km); ferry range (with 2,265 Imp gal/10 296 l of external fuel), 5,354 mls (8 617 km).

Weights: Operational empty, 79,516 lb (36 068 kg); max take-off, 155,000 lb (70 310 kg).

Accommodation: Normal flight crew of four and provision for 97 casualty litters plus medical attendants, 128 combat troops or 92 paratroops. For pure freight role up to seven cargo pallets may be loaded. Some 105 of the total number of Hercules delivered have been supplied for commercial operation.

Status: A total of 1,750 Hercules (all versions) against orders for 1,800 had been delivered by the beginning of 1986 when production was continuing at three monthly.

Notes: The L-100-30 and its military equivalent, the C-130H-30, are stretched versions of the basic Hercules, the C-130H. The original civil model, the L-100-20 featured a 100-in (2,54-m) fuselage stretch over the basic military model, and the L-100-30, intended for both military and civil application, embodies a further 80-in (2,03-m) stretch. Military operators of the C-130H-30 version are Algeria, Indonesia, Ecuador, Cameroun and Nigeria, and 30 of the RAF's Hercules C Mk 1s (equivalent of the C-130H) have been modified to C-130H-30 standards as Hercules C Mk 3s. Some 40 variants of the Hercules have so far been produced and this type now serves (in military and civil roles) with 56 countries.

LOCKHEED L-100-30 HERCULES

Dimensions: Span, 132 ft 7 in (40,41 m); length, 112 ft 9 in (34,37 m); height, 38 ft 3 in (11,66 m); wing area, 1,745 sq ft (162,12 m²).

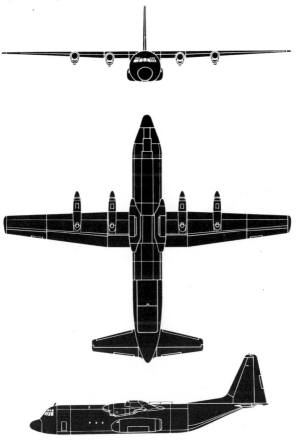

LOCKHEED P-3C ORION

Country of Origin: USA.

Type: Long-range maritime patrol aircraft.

Power Plant: Four 4,910 eshp Allison T56-A-14W turbo-props.

Performance: Max speed (at 105,000 lb/47 625 kg), 473 mph (761 km/h) at 15,000 ft (4 570 m); cruise, 397 mph (639 km/h) at 25,000 ft (7 620 m); patrol speed, 230 mph (370 km/h) at 1,500 ft (460 m); loiter endurance (all engines) at 1,500 ft (460 m), 12·3 hrs, (two engines), 17 hrs; mission radius 2,530 mls (4 075 km), (with three hours on station at 1,500 ft/460 m), 1,933 mls (3 110 km).

Weights: Empty, 61,491 lb (27 890 kg); normal loaded, 133,500 lb (60 558 kg); max overload take-off, 142,000 lb (64 410 kg).

Accommodation: Normal flight crew of 10 including five in tactical compartment.

Armament: Two Mk 101 depth bombs and four Mk 43, 44 or 46 torpedoes, or eight Mk 54 bombs in weapons bay, and provision for up to 13,713 lb (6 220 kg) of external ordnance.

Status: Prototype (YP-3C) flown 8 October 1968, with deliveries to the US Navy (of P-3C Update III) continuing at beginning of 1986 against total requirement of 287 (P-3Cs) and under licence (by Kawasaki) for Japanese Maritime Self-Defence Force with 23 delivered against total requirement for 100 aircraft.

Notes: The P-3C followed 157 P-3As and 125 P-3Bs, and has been supplied to the RAAF (20), Iran (six as P-3Fs), the Canadian Armed Forces (18 as CP-140 Auroras) and the Netherlands (13), one of the last-mentioned being illustrated above, in addition to Japan. Deliveries of the current Update III version began in May 1984. An airborne early warning and control system version (1985 edition) is under development.

LOCKHEED P-3C ORION

Dimensions: Span, 99 ft 8 in (30,37 m); length, 116 ft 10 in (35,61 m); height, 33 ft 8½ in (10,29 m); wing area, 1,300 sq ft (120,77 m²).

LOCKHEED (MCE) TRISTAR K MK 1

Country of Origin: United Kingdom (USA).
Type: Flight refuelling tanker and military freighter.
Power Plant: Three 50,000 lb st (22 680 kgp) Rolls-Royce RB.211-524B4 turbofans.
Performance: Max cruising speed, 599 mph (964 km/h) at 35,000 ft (10 670 m); long-range cruise (typical), 552 mph (889 km/h) or Mach=0·83 at 33,000 ft (10 060 m); range (with max payload), 4,834 mls (7 780 km) with reserves for 345 mls (555 km) and one hour at 5,000 ft (1 525 m).
Weights: Typical empty (tanker), 242,864 lb (110 163 kg), (tanker/freighter), 244,710 lb (111 000 kg); max take-off, 540,000 lb (245 000 kg).
Accommodation: Flight crew of three with 12-seat crew rest area and (personnel transportation) 204 passengers basically 10 abreast in main cabin, with total baggage capacity of 25,080 lb (11 376 kg) in 33 containers. (KC Mk 1) One hundred and ninety-four passengers with three baggage pallets, 182 passengers with four pallets or 157 passengers with six pallets. As tanker max fuel capacity of 213,240 lb (96 726 kg).
Status: Six ex-British Airways TriStars being modified for RAF by Marshall of Cambridge (Engineering) of which first flown as K Mk 1 on 9 July 1985. Fifth and sixth aircraft to be completed as KC Mk 1 tanker/freighters, and first and second aircraft subsequently to be modified to same standard. Three ex-Pan Am aircraft to be converted as K Mk 2s.
Notes: The TriStar KC Mk 1, a military conversion of the TriStar commercial transport (see 1982 edition), will differ from the K Mk 1 in having forward freight-loading doors and a cargo handling system.

LOCKHEED (MCE) TRISTAR K MK 1

Dimensions: Span, 164 ft 6 in (50,09 m); length (excluding probe), 164 ft $2\frac{1}{2}$ in (50,05 m); height, 55 ft 4 in (16,87 m); wing area, 3,541 sq ft (329,0 m²).

McDONNELL DOUGLAS F-15C EAGLE

Country of Origin: USA.

Type: Single-seat air superiority fighter.

Power Plant: Two 14,780 lb st (6705 kgp) dry and 23,904 lb st (10855 kgp) reheat Pratt & Whitney F100-PW-100 turbofans.

Performance: Max speed (short-endurance dash), 1,676 mph (2698 km/h) or Mach=2·54, (sustained), 1,518 mph (2443 km/h) or Mach=2·3 at 40,000 ft (12190 m); max endurance (internal fuel), 2·9 hrs, (with conformal pallets), 5·25 hrs; service ceiling, 63,000 ft (19 200 m).

Weights: Basic equipped, 28,700 lb (13 018 kg); loaded (full internal fuel and four AIM-7 AAMs), 44,500 lb (20 185 kg); max take-off, 68,000 lb (30 845 kg).

Armament: One 20-mm M-61A1 rotary cannon plus four AIM-7F Sparrow and four AIM-9L Sidewinder AAMs.

Status: First flown 26 February 1979, the F-15C is the second major single-seat production version of the Eagle, having, together with its two-seat equivalent, the F-15D, supplanted the F-15A and F-15B from the 444th aircraft mid 1980. The F-15C and D were the current production models at the beginning of 1986, with more than 900 (all versions) delivered, total USAF Eagle requirement being 1,488 aircraft, including 392 of the dual-role two-seat F-15E for delivery from 1988.

Notes: Featuring upgraded avionics and conformal fuel packs, the F-15C has been supplied to Saudi Arabia (47 plus 15 F-15Ds) and 177 are being licence manufactured as F-15Js by Japan (including eight from knocked-down assemblies) which country also received 12 F-15DJ two-seaters. Israel received 40 F-15 Eagles (since modified for conformal tanks) and is to receive a further 11 aircraft. The F-15C illustrated above is fitted with the LANTIRN (Low Altitude Navigation and Targeting Infrared for Night) system to be standardised by the F-15E which will enter test December 1986.

McDONNELL DOUGLAS F-15C EAGLE

Dimensions: Span, 42 ft 9¾ in (13,05 m); length, 63 ft 9 in (19,43 m); height, 18 ft 5½ in (5,63 m); wing area, 608 sq ft (56,50 m²).

McDONNELL DOUGLAS F/A-18A HORNET

Country of Origin: USA.

Type: Single-seat shipboard and shore-based multi-role fighter and attack aircraft.

Power Plant: Two 10,600 lb st (4810 kgp) dry and 15,800 lb st (7167 kgp) reheat General Electric F404-GE-400 turbofans.

Performance: Max speed (AAMs on wingtip and fuselage stations), 1,190 mph (1915 km/h) or Mach = 1·8 at 40,000 ft (12150 m); initial climb (half fuel and wingtip AAMs), 60,000 ft/min (304,6 m/sec); tactical radius (combat air patrol on internal fuel), 480 mls (770 km), (with three 262 Imp gal/1192 l external tanks), 735 mls (1180 km).

Weights: Empty equipped, 28,000 lb (12700 kg); loaded (air superiority mission with half fuel and four AAMs), 35,800 lb (16240 kg); max take-off, 56,000 lb (25400 kg).

Armament: One 20-mm M-61A-1 rotary cannon and (air-air) two AIM-7E/F Sparrow and two AIM-9G/H Sidewinder AAMs, or (attack) up to 17,000 lb (7711 kg) of ordnance.

Status: First of 11 FSD (full-scale development) Hornets (including two TF-18A two-seaters) flown 18 November 1978. Planning at beginning of 1986 called for 1,366 Hornets for US Navy and US Marine Corps (including 153 TF-18As). First production F/A-18A flown April 1980.

Notes: Land-based versions of the Hornet have been ordered by Australia (57 F/A-18As and 18 TF-18As), Canada (113 CF-18As and 24 CF-18Bs) and Spain (72 EF-18As and TF-18As). Separate F-18 fighter and A-18 attack versions of the Hornet were initially planned by the US Navy. Both roles were subsequently combined in a single basic version, and current planning calls for the inclusion of two Hornet squadrons in the complement of each of the large US Navy carriers. The RF-18 replaces the 20-mm gun with a sensor pallet.

McDONNELL DOUGLAS F/A-18A HORNET

Dimensions: Span, 37 ft 6 in (11,43 m); length, 56 ft 0 in (17,07 m); height, 15 ft 4 in (4,67 m); wing area, 396 sq ft (36,79 m²).

McDONNELL DOUGLAS KC-10A EXTENDER

Country of Origin: USA.

Type: Flight refuelling tanker and military freighter.

Power Plant: Three 52,500 lb st (23 814 kgp) General Electric CF6-50C2 turbofans.

Performance: Max speed, 620 mph (988 km/h) at 33,000 ft (10 060 m); max cruise, 595 mph (957 km/h) at 31,000 ft (9 450 m); long-range cruise, 540 mph (870 km/h); typical refuelling mission, 2,200 mls (3 540 km) from base with 200,000 lb (90 720 kg) of fuel and return; max range (with 170,000 lb/77 112 kg freight), 4,370 mls (7 033 km).

Weights: Operational empty (tanker), 239,747 lb (108 749 kg), (cargo configuration), 243,973 lb (110 660 kg); max take-off, 590,000 lb (267 624 kg).

Accommodation: Flight crew of five plus provision for six seats for additional crew and four bunks for crew rest. Fourteen further seats may be provided for support personnel in the forward cabin. Alternatively, a larger area can be provided for 55 more support personnel, with necessary facilities, to increase total accommodation (including flight crew) to 80.

Status: First KC-10A was flown on 12 July 1980, with 16 ordered by the USAF by the beginning of 1983. A further 44 have been ordered under five-year contracting process for delivery through 1987. First operational KC-10A squadron was activated on 1 October 1981, and 38 had been delivered to the USAF by the beginning of 1986.

Notes: The KC-10A is a military tanker/freighter derivative of the commercial DC-10 Series 30 (see 1983 edition) with refuelling boom, boom operator's station, hose and drogue, and body fuel cells in the lower cargo compartments. When current contracts are fulfilled, 20 KC-10A Extenders will be assigned to each of the Barksdale, March and Seymour Johnson Air Force Bases.

McDONNELL DOUGLAS KC-10A EXTENDER

Dimensions: Span, 165 ft 4 in (50,42 m); length, 182 ft 0 in (55,47 m); height, 58 ft 1 in (17,70 m); wing area, 3,958 sq ft (367,7 m²).

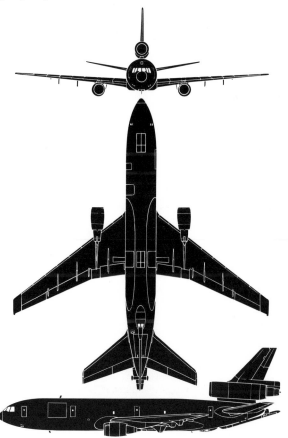

McDONNELL DOUGLAS MD-80

Country of Origin: USA.

Type: Short/medium-haul commercial airliner.

Power Plant: (MD-81) Two 19,250lbst (8730kgp) Pratt & Whitney JT8D-209 turbofans.

Performance: Max cruising speed, 574mph (924km/h) at 27,000ft (8230m); econ cruise, 522mph (840km/h) at 33,000ft (10060m); long-range cruise, 505mph (813km/h) at 35,000ft (10670m); range (with max payload), 1,594mls (2565km) at econ cruise, (with max fuel), 3,280mls (5280km) at long-range cruise.

Weights: Operational empty, 77,797lb (35289kg); max take-off, 140,000lb (63503kg).

Accommodation: Flight crew of two and typical mixed-class arrangement for 23 first- and 137 economy-class passengers, or 155 all-economy or 172 commuter-type arrangements with five-abreast seating.

Status: First MD-80 flown (as Super 80) on 18 October 1979, with first customer delivery (to Swissair) on 12 September 1980, and some 580 orders and options by beginning of 1986 with 260 delivered, production being 7·25 monthly.

Notes: The MD-80 is the largest of six members of the DC-9 family, the MD-82 sub-type having 20,850lbst (9458kgp) JT8D-217 engines with which it was certificated at a max take-off weight of 149,500lb (67813kg) in September 1982, this giving a max payload range of 2,300mls (3700km). The MD-83 with a max take-off weight of 160,000lb (72576kg) and a max payload range of the order of 2,880mls (4630km), was flown on 17 December 1984. Overall size remains unchanged. The MD-87, launched at the beginning of 1985 for 1986 delivery, has a 17ft 5in (5,30m) shorter fuselage, JT8D-217B engines and capacity for 130–139 passengers.

McDONNELL DOUGLAS MD-80

Dimension: Span, 107 ft 10 in (32,85 m); length, 147 ft 10 in (45,08 m); height, 29 ft 4 in (8,93 m); wing area, 1,279 sq ft (118,8 m²).

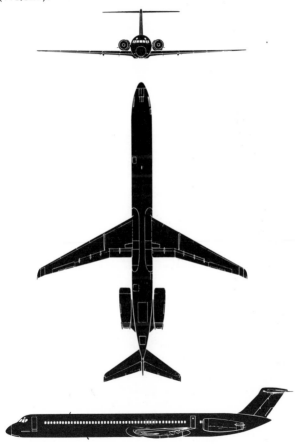

MIKOYAN MIG-23 (FLOGGER)

Country of Origin: USSR.

Type: (Flogger-G) Single-seat counterair fighter.

Power Plant: One 17,635 lb st (8 000 kgp) dry and 25,350 lb st (11 500 kgp) reheat Tumansky R-29B turbojet.

Performance: (Flogger-G) Max speed (clean aircraft with 50% fuel), 1,520 mph (2 446 km/h) above 36,100 ft (11 000 m) or Mach = 2·3; combat radius (high-altitude air-air mission with four AAMs), 530 mls (850 km), (with centreline combat tank), 700 mls.

Weights: (Flogger-G) Normal loaded (clean), 34,170 lb (15 500 kg); max take-off, 44,312 lb (20 100 kg).

Armament: (Flogger-G) One 23-mm twin-barrel GSh-23L cannon and two R-23R Apex and two R-60 Aphid AAMs.

Status: Aerodynamic prototype of MiG-23 flown 1966–67, and first major production model (Flogger-B) entering service in 1972, being succeeded in production for the air-air role by upgraded version (Flogger-G) 1977–78. Production continuing at rate of 25–30 monthly (all versions) at beginning of 1986 when it remained the most numerous of fighters in the current Soviet inventory.

Notes: The MiG-23 has evolved as a family of aircraft of which the Flogger-G (described and illustrated) is the latest air-air version. The Flogger-E is an export equivalent of the earlier Flogger-B, and the Flogger-F and -H are air-ground versions with a similar forward fuselage to that of the MiG-27 (see 1985 edition), a dedicated tactical strike and close air support fighter which, in its Flogger-J version, is currently being licence-built in India. The MiG-23 is currently operated by the air forces of all WarPac countries and has been supplied to the air forces of at least eight other countries. Most of these include in their inventories the tandem two-seat MiG-23UM trainer which is combat capable.

MIKOYAN MIG-23 (FLOGGER)

Dimensions: (Estimated) Span (17 deg sweep), 46 ft 9 in (14,25 m), 72 deg sweep), 27 ft 6 in (8,38 m); length (including probe), 55 ft 1½ in (16,80 m); wing area, 293·4 sq ft (27,26 m²).

MIKOYAN MIG-29 (FULCRUM)

Country of Origin: USSR.

Type: Single-seat counterair fighter.

Power Plant: Two 11,243 lb st (5 100 kgp) dry and 18,300 lb st (8 300 kgp) reheat Tumansky R-33D turbofans.

Performance: (Estimated) Max speed (four air-air missiles and 50% fuel), 1,518 mph (2 445 km/h) above 36,100 ft (11 000 m) or Mach=2·3, 915 mph (1 470 km/h) at sea level or Mach=1·2; max initial climb, 50,000 ft/min (254 m/sec); combat radius (air-air mission with four AAMs), 415 mls (670 km), (secondary attack mission with four 1,100-lb/500-kg bombs), 375 mls (600 km).

Weights: (Estimated) Operational empty, 18,000 lb (8 165 kg); max take-off, 36,000 lb (16 330 kg).

Armament: One 30-mm cannon and two R-23R (Apex) and four R-60 Aphid AAMs, or six AA-10 medium-range AAMs.

Status: First seen in prototype form in 1979, the MiG-29 attained initial operational capability with the Soviet Air Forces in 1984, and about 100 aircraft of this type were expected to be in service by the beginning of 1986. Forty have been ordered by the Indian Air Force which anticipated receiving the first batch (six single-seaters and two two-seaters) in November 1985.

Notes: Possessing an essentially similar configuration to that of the larger and heavier Su-27, the MiG-29 features long-range track-while-scan radar, a pulse-Doppler lookdown/shootdown weapon system, infrared search and tracking, and a digital data link. The Indian government is negotiating a manufacturing licence for the MiG-29, preliminary planning calling for the production of 150 by HAL commencing in 1988. A two-seat version of the MiG-29 for conversion training is combat capable.

154

MIKOYAN MIG-29 (FULCRUM)

Dimensions: (Estimated) Span, 34 ft 5 in (10,50 m); length (including probe), 50 ft 10 in (15,50 m); height, 17 ft 2 in (5,25 m); wing area, 380 sq ft (35,30 m²).

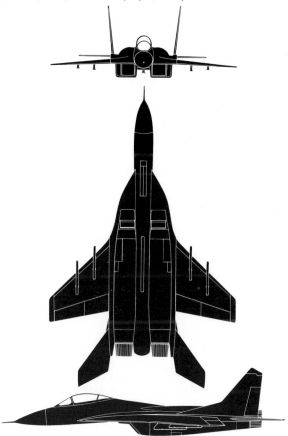

MIKOYAN MIG-31 (FOXHOUND)

Country of Origin: USSR.

Type: Tandem two-seat interceptor fighter.

Power Plant: Two 30,865 lb st (14 000 kgp) reheat Tumansky turbojets.

Performance: (Estimated) Max speed, 1,520 mph (2 445 km/h) above 36,100 ft (11 000 m), or Mach = 2·3, 915 mph (1 472 km/h) at sea level; max operational radius (with external fuel), 1,180 mls (1 900 km); ceiling 80,000 ft (24 385 m).

Weights: (Estimated) Empty equipped, 45,000 lb (20 410 kg); normal loaded, 65,200 lb (29 575 kg)

Armament: Up to eight AA-9 radar-guided AAMs.

Status: The MiG-31 has been under development since the mid 'seventies and is believed to have been first deployed in 1982, with several regiments equipped with this type by the beginning of 1986 when some 90 were operational.

Notes: The MiG-31 has been derived from the MiG-25 (see 1984 Edition) and features a redesigned forward fuselage housing a lookdown-shootdown pulse Doppler weapons system and tandem cockpits for the pilot and systems operator. Some indication of the capability of the MiG-31 came in 1978, when a Soviet official announcement indicated that, during tests, presumably a prototype flying at around 6 000 m (19 685 ft) had detected a target flying below 60 m (200 ft) at a range of 20 km (12·5 mls), fired an unarmed missile against it and achieved a theoretical kill. The Tumansky engines installed in the MiG-31 are fundamentally similar to those employed by the MiG-25 derivative, referred to as the Ye-266M, which established a series of world height records.

MIKOYAN MIG-31 (FOXHOUND)

Dimensions: (Estimated) Span, 45 ft 9 in (13,94 m); length, 68 ft 10 in (21,00 m); height, 18 ft 6 in (5,63 m); wing area, 602·8 sq ft (56,00 m²).

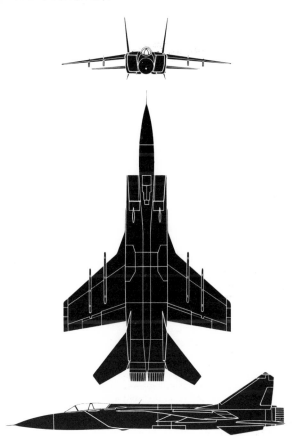

NANCHANG QIANG-5 (FANTAN-A)

Country of Origin: China.

Type: Single-seat close air support and ground attack aircraft.

Power Plant: Two 5,732 lb st (2 600 kgp) dry and 7,165 lb st (3 250 kgp) reheat Shenyang Wopen-6C turbojets.

Performance: Max speed (at 21,010 lb/9 530 kg), 740 mph (1 190 km/h) or Mach = 1·12 at 36,000 ft (10 975 m), 752 mph (1 210 km/h) or Mach = 0·987 at sea level; combat radius (with 4,410 lb/2 000 kg external stores), 248 mls (400 km) LO-LO-LO, 373 mls (600 km) HI-LO-HI; max range (with two 167 imp gal/760 l drop tanks), 1,224 mls (1 970 km).

Weights: Empty, 14,317 lb (6 494 kg); loaded (clean), 21,010 lb (9 530 kg); max take-off, 26,455 lb (12 000 kg).

Armament: Two 23-mm cannon plus 4,410 lb (2 000 kg) ordnance distributed between eight hardpoints (six wing and two fuselage).

Status: The Qiang-5 (Q-5) apparently entered flight test in the mid 'seventies, and at least 200 were allegedly in Chinese service by 1979, production having since continued at Nanchang both for China and for export (as the A-5) in progressively improved versions of which the latest is designated A-5C. The first export customer was Pakistan to which deliveries of an initial batch of 42 began in 1983. (An example in service with Pakistan being illustrated above.)

Notes: The Qiang-5 is a derivative of the Jian-6 (J-6), which, in turn, was a copy of the Soviet MiG-19SF, and is currently being marketed (as the A-5C) through Singapore's Aerospace Industries. Early versions of the Qiang-5 featured an internal weapons bay, but current models have deleted this feature in favour of increased internal fuel capacity. The Wopen-6C (WP-6C) engines are essentially similar to the Tumansky R-9BF-811.

NANCHANG QIANG-5 (FANTAN-A)

Dimensions: Span, 31 ft 10 in (9,70 m); length (excluding nose probe), 51 ft 4⅛ in (15,65 m); height, 14 ft 9½ in (4,51 m); wing area, 300·85 sq ft (27,95 m²).

NORMAN NAC 1 FREELANCE

Country of Origin: United Kingdom.
Type: Light cabin monoplane.
Power Plant: One 180 hp Avco Lycoming IO-360-A3A four-cylinder horizontally-opposed engine.
Performance: Max speed, 140 mph (225 km/h) at sea level; cruise (75% power), 135 mph (217 km/h) at sea level; max initial climb, 700 ft/min (3,6 m/sec); service ceiling, 17,000 ft (5 180 m); max range (no reserves and 75% power), 960 mls (1 545 km).
Weights: Empty equipped, 1,400 lb (613 kg); max take-off, 2,450 lb (1 114 kg).
Accommodation: Pilot and three passengers in side-by-side pairs of individual seats.
Status: Prototype first flown on 29 September 1984, with certification planned for 1987, and production of 20–25 annually anticipated from 1988.
Notes: Built by NDN Aircraft for the Norman Aeroplane Company, the NAC 1 Freelance is a derivative of the BN-3 Nymph flown on 17 May 1969 (see 1970 edition), but has a more powerful engine, a new wing section, flaps and ailerons of different structure, increased fuel capacity of integral type, revised wing bracing, and various more minor improvements. A feature of the aeroplane is its aft-folding wings. These can be folded "within 30 seconds of engine shutdown" and allow the Freelance to be accommodated in a space 23 ft 6 in (7,16 m) long by 12 ft (3,66 m) wide. A 100 US gal (379 l) detachable spray tank with booms and nozzle or Micronair atomiser rigs may be attached beneath the fuselage.

NORMAN NAC 1 FREELANCE

Dimensions: Span, 39 ft 4 in (11,98 m); length, 23 ft 7¾ in (7,20 m); height, 9 ft 6 in (2,90 m); wing area, 169 sq ft (15,70 m²).

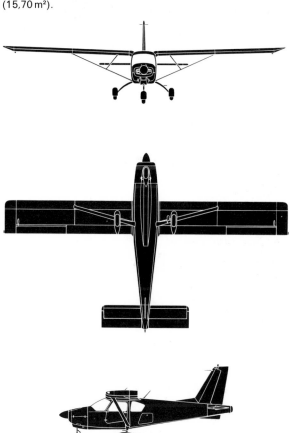

NORMAN NDN 6 FIELDMASTER

Country of Origin: United Kingdom.
Type: Two-seat agricultural aircraft.
Power Plant: One 750 hp Pratt & Whitney Canada PT6A-34AG turboprop.
Performance: Max speed (clean), 157 mph (253 km/h) at 5,500 ft (1 675 m); max cruise, 155 mph (250 km/h) at sea level; max initial climb (at 10,000 lb/4 536 kg), 600 ft/min (3,05 m/sec); range (two crew and 1,000 lb/453·6 kg of equipment), 806 mls (1 297 km).
Weights: Empty equipped (typical), 4,570 lb (2 154 kg); max take-off, 10,000 ib (4 536 kg).
Status: Prototype Fieldmaster flown on 17 December 1981. Production expected to commence during 1986, with five aircraft to be completed by June 1987, and 1·5 aircraft monthly from 1988.
Notes: Claimed to be the first agricultural aircraft designed from the outset for turboprop power, the Fieldmaster will normally be flown as a single-seater, but accommodation is provided for a second person (eg, mechanic/loader, pupil pilot or fire spotter). The Fieldmaster can be utilised as a firebomber with a water scoop and boom extending along the underside of the rear fuselage and lowered to take on water (as seen above) by means of a winch. The integral titanium hopper/tank (which has a capacity of 581 Imp gal/2 642 l) is part of the primary structure and carries the engine bearers at its forward end and the rear fuselage with cockpit aft.

162

NORMAN NDN 6 FIELDMASTER

Dimensions: Span, 50 ft 3 in (15,32 m); length, 36 ft 2 in (10,97 m); height, 12 ft 3 in (3,73 m); wing area, 338 sq ft (31,42 m²).

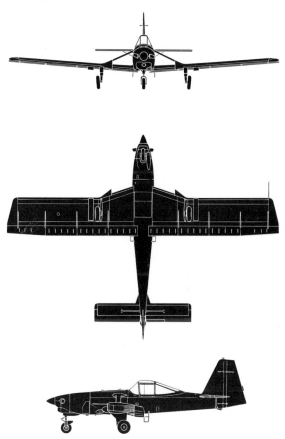

NORTHROP F-20A TIGERSHARK

Country of Origin: USA.
Type: Single-seat multi-role fighter.
Power Plant: One 17,000 lb st (7 711 kgp) reheat General Electric F404-GE-100 turbofan.
Performance: Max speed, 1,320 mph (2 124 km/h) or Mach 2·0 above 36,000 ft (10 975 m), 800 mph (1 288 km/h) or Mach 1·05 at sea level; initial climb at combat weight (50% internal fuel and wingtip missiles), 52,800 ft/min (268,2 m/sec); combat ceiling, 54,700 ft (16 672 m); time to 40,000 ft (12 190 m) from brakes release, 2·3 min; tactical radius with two 229 Imp gal/1 040 l drop tanks and 20 min reserve at sea level (HI-LO-HI interdiction with seven Mk 82 bombs), 437 mls (704 km), (combat air patrol with 96 min on station), 345 mls (555 km); ferry range (max fuel), 1,842 mls (2 965 km).
Weights: Take-off (wingtip missiles), 18,345 lb (8 321 kg); max take-off, 27,502 lb (12 475 kg).
Armament: Two 20-mm M-39 cannon and up to 7,000 lb (3 175 kg) of external ordnance on five stations.
Status: Prototypes of the F-20 were flown on 30 August 1982, 26 August 1983 and 12 May 1984, with fourth prototype (in fully operational configuration) to fly in 1986.
Notes: The Tigershark is an advanced derivative of the F-5E Tiger II (see 1981 edition) with a low-bypass turbofan affording 70 per cent more thrust than the twin engines of the earlier fighter, integrated digital avionics, including a digital flight control system, and a multi-mode coherent pulse-Doppler radar. The fourth prototype will be completed in the proposed operational configuration, with an 18,000 lb st (8 165 kgp) F404 engine, 650 lb (295 kg) more internal fuel, a larger radar antenna and redesigned leading and trailing edge flaps.

NORTHROP F-20A TIGERSHARK

Dimensions: Span, 26 ft 8 in (8,13 m); length, 46 ft 6 in (14,17 m); height, 13 ft 10 in (4,22 m); wing area, 186 sq ft (17,28 m²).

PANAVIA TORNADO F MK 3

Country of Origin: United Kingdom.
Type: Tandem two-seat air defence interceptor.
Power Plant: Two (approx) 9,000 lb st (4 082 kgp) dry and 17,000 lb st (7 711 kgp) reheat Turbo-Union RB.199-34R Mk 104 turbofans.
Performance: (Estimated) Max speed, 920 mph (1 480 km/h) or Mach=1·2 at sea level, 1,450 mph (2 333 km/h) Or Mach=2·2 at 40,000 ft (12 190 m); time to 30,000 ft (9 145 m), 1·7 min; operational radius (combat air patrol with two 330 Imp gal/1 500 l drop tanks and allowance for 2 hrs loiter), 350–450 mls (560–725 km); ferry range (with four 330 Imp gal/1 400 l external tanks), 2,650 mls (4 265 km).
Weights: (Estimated) Empty equipped, 31,970 lb (14 500 kg); normal loaded (four Sky Flash and four AIM-9L AAMs), 50,700 lb (30 000 kg); max, 56,000 lb (25 400 kg).
Armament: One 27-mm IWKA-Mauser cannon plus four BAe Sky Flash and four AIM-9L Sidewinder AAMs.
Status: First of three F Mk 2 prototypes flown on 27 October 1979, and first of 18 production F Mk 2s (including six F Mk 2Ts) flown 5 March 1984. Deliveries of F Mk 3s (against RAF requirement for 147) commencing early 1986. Eight ordered by Oman and 24 by Saudi Arabia.
Notes: The Tornado F Mk 3 is the definitive air defence version for the RAF of the multi-national (UK, Federal Germany and Italy) multi-role fighter (see 1978 edition). It differs from the Mk 2 in having Mk 104 engines with 14-in (36-cm) reheat pipe extensions and provision for four rather than two AIM-9L Sidewinders.

PANAVIA TORNADO F MK 3

Dimensions: Span (25 deg sweep), 45 ft 7¼ in (13,90 m), (68 deg sweep), 28 ft 2½ in (8,59 m); Length, 59 ft 3 in (18,06 m); height, 18 ft 8½ in (5,70 m); wing area, 322·9 sq ft (30,00 m²).

PILATUS PC-9

Country of Origin: Switzerland.

Type: Tandem two-seat basic/advanced trainer.

Power Plant: One 950 shp Pratt & Whitney Canada PT6A-62 turboprop.

Performance: Max speed, 308 mph (496 km/h) at sea level, 345 mph (556 km/h) at 20,000 ft (6 100 m); max initial climb, 4,050 ft/min (20,6 m/sec); service ceiling, 38,000 ft (11 580 m); max range (5 per cent plus 20 min reserves), 690 mls (1 111 km) at 10,000 ft (3 050 m), 955 mls (1 538 km) at 20,000 ft (6 100 m).

Weights: Empty, 3,715 lb (1 685 kg); max take-off (clean) 4,960 lb (2 250 kg), (with external stores), 6,834 lb (3 100 kg).

Status: First and second prototypes flown on 7 May and 20 July 1984, with certification following in August 1985. The first series PC-9 was scheduled for completion in November 1985, at which time an order had been placed by Burma, and Saudi Arabia had signed a Memorandum of Understanding concerning the procurement of 30 PC-9s via British Aerospace.

Notes: The PC-9 bears a close external resemblance to the PC-7 (see 1984 edition), but is, in fact, a very different design, with only about 10 per cent structural commonality with the earlier trainer. Differences include a more powerful engine (flat-rated from 1,150 shp), the provision of vertically-staggered ejection seats, modified wing profiles and tips, new ailerons and a ventral air brake. The PC-9s to be procured for the Royal Saudi Air Force are to be purchased from Pilatus by British Aerospace, the latter being responsible for the installation of cockpits closely compatible with those of the BAe Hawk.

Dimensions: Span, 33 ft 2½ in (10,12 m); length, 33 ft 4 in (10,17 m); height, 10 ft 8⅓ in (3,26 m); wing area, 175·3 sq ft (16,29 m²).

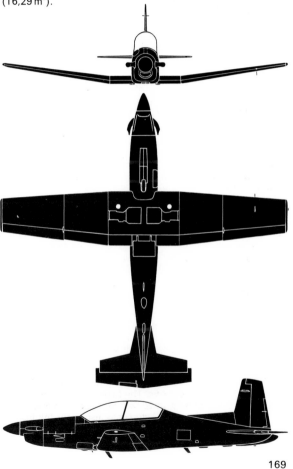

PIPER PA-46-310P MALIBU

Country of Origin: USA.

Type: Light cabin monoplane.

Power Plant: One 310 hp Continental TSIO-520-BE six-cylinder horizontally-opposed engine.

Performance: Max speed, 254 mph (409 km/h) at optimum altitude; cruise (75% power), 239 mph (385 km/h), 65% power), 225 mph (363 km/h); initial climb, 1,143 ft/min (5,8 m/sec); range (with 45 min reserves), 1,542 mls (2 482 km) at 75% power, 1,657 mls (2 667 km) at 65% power, 1,830 mls (2 945 km) at 55% power.

Weights: Standard empty, 2,275 lb (1 032 kg); max take-off, 3,850 lb (1 746 kg).

Accommodation: Pilot and five passengers in paired individual seats with rear airstair door.

Status: First prototype Malibu flown late 1980, with production prototype flying in August 1982. Certification was obtained in September 1983, with customer deliveries commencing in the following November. More than 200 delivered by beginning of 1986 when production rate was 8–9 monthly.

Notes: Intended to compete with the Cessna P210 Centurion, which, prior to the advent of the Malibu, was the sole pressurised single-engined cabin monoplane on the market, this new Piper aircraft is claimed to be the first production single-engined general aviation model to utilise computer-aided design and manufacturing (CAD/CAM) techniques. Possessing no relationship to previous Piper designs, the Malibu offers a cabin of "business twin" proportions with club seating and a rear airstair door, and is designed to give an 8,000 ft (2 440 m) cabin pressure up to 25,000 ft (7 620 m). At the end of 1985, Piper was considering a turboprop conversion of the Malibu.

PIPER PA-46-310P MALIBU

Dimensions: Span, 43 ft 0 in (13,10 m); length, 28 ft 4¾ in (8,66 m); height, 11 ft 3½ in (3,44 m); wing area, 175 sq ft (16,26 m²).

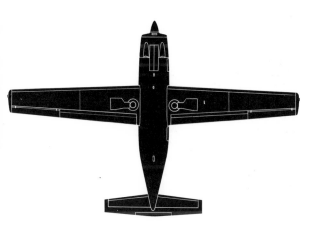

PZL-130 ORLIK

Country of Origin: Poland.

Type: Tandem two-seat primary/basic trainer.

Power Plant: One 330 hp Vedeneev M-14Pm nine-cylinder radial air-cooled engine.

Performance: (At 2,866 lb/1 300 kg) Max speed, 239 mph (385 km/h); max continuous cruise, 224 mph (360 km/h); initial climb, 1,457 ft/min (7,4 m/sec); service ceiling, 22,965 ft (7 000 m); max range, 1,392 mls.

Weights: Empty equipped, 2,088 lb (947 kg) max take-off, 3,307 lb (1 500 kg).

Status: First of three flying prototypes entered flight test on 12 October 1984, with second and third following on 29 December 1984 and 12 January 1985 respectively. Work on a pre-series of 10 aircraft was proceeding at the beginning of 1986.

Notes: The Orlik (Eaglet) has been designed as the primary component of the so-called Kolegium System, the other components being a flight simulator and an electronic diagnostic device intended to facilitate servicing by automatic diagnosis of engine and system faults. Intended for use by the Polish Air Force from *ab initio* instruction through to jet conversion, the Orlik features a low aspect ratio wing which permits simulation of the roll yaw characteristics and low speed sink rates typical of high-performance combat aircraft. A turboprop-powered version, the Orlik-Turbo, is projected, this having a flat-rated 550 shp Pratt & Whitney Canada PT6A-25A engine and being intended solely for export. The Polish Air Force reportedly requires in excess of 200 Orliks.

PZL-130 ORLIK

Dimensions: Span, 26 ft 3 in (8,00 m); length, 27 ft 9 in (8,45 m); height, 13 ft 1½ in (4,00 m); wing area, 132·4 sq ft (12,30 m²).

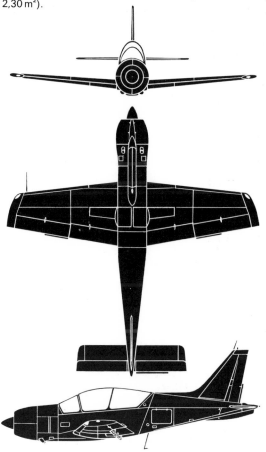

RHEIN-FLUGZEUGBAU FANTRAINER

Country of Origin: Federal Germany.

Type: Tandem two-seat primary/basic trainer.

Power Plant: One (Fantrainer 400) 420 shp Allison 250-C20B or (Fantrainer 600) 600 shp Allison 250-C30 turboshaft driving a five-bladed ducted fan.

Performance: (Fantrainer 400) Max speed, 230 mph (370 km/h) at 10,000 ft (3 050 m); initial climb, 2,000 ft/min (10,2 m/sec); range (no reserves), 1,094 mls (1 760 km). (Fantrainer 600) Max speed, 267 mph (430 km/h) at 18,000 ft (5 485 m); initial climb, 3,150 ft/min (16 m/sec); range (no reserves), 863 mls (1 390 km).

Weights: (Fantrainer 400) Empty, 2,456 lb (1 114 kg); max take-off, 3,968 lb (1 800 kg). (Fantrainer 600) Empty 2,557 lb (1 160 kg); max take-off, 5,071 lb (2 300 kg).

Status: First of two prototypes flown 27 October 1977, and first production aircraft (Fantrainer 600) flown on 12 August 1984. The Royal Thai Air Force has ordered 31 Fantrainer 400s and 16 Fantrainer 600s, and has an option on a further 26 Fantrainer 600s, deliveries to Thailand having commenced in October 1984.

Notes: First two aircraft for Thailand shipped in flyaway condition and remainder being supplied as major component kits for assembly in Thailand with locally-manufactured wings, the workshare between RFB and Thailand progressively increasing from a ratio of 80:20 to 57:43. The Fantrainer 600 has been modified in Thailand to carry a pod-mounted 20-mm cannon. Of unconventional design, the Fantrainer minimises transition problems by simulating pure jet flight. The Fantrainer was originally selected by the *Luftwaffe* as a replacement for the P. 149D trainer, but the programme was discontinued owing to funding difficulties. However, re-evaluation of the Fantrainer was being undertaken by the *Luftwaffe* late in 1985.

RHEIN-FLUGZEUGBAU FANTRAINER

Dimensions: Span, 31 ft 10 in (9,70 m); length, 30 ft 3½ in (9,23 m); height, 9 ft 10 in (3,00 m); wing area, 149·6 sq ft (13,90 m²).

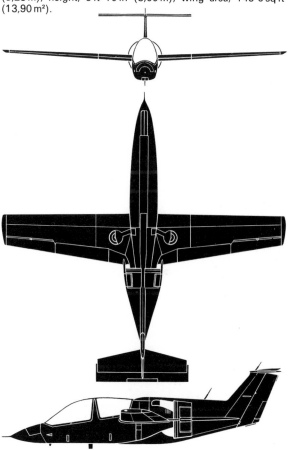

ROCKWELL B-1B

Country of Origin: USA.
Type: Strategic bomber and cruise missile carrier.
Power Plant: Four 30,750 lb st (13 948 kgp) General Electric F101-GE-102 turbofans.
Performance: Max speed (clean condition), 792 mph (1 275 km/h) or Mach = 1·2 at 40,000 ft (12 190 m); low-level penetration speed, 610 mph (980 km/h) or Mach = 0·8.
Weights: Empty, 179,985 lb (81 641 kg); max take-off, 477,000 lb (216 367 kg).
Accommodation: Flight crew of four comprising pilot, co-pilot and offensive and defensive systems operators.
Armament: Eight AGM-86B cruise missiles and 12 AGM-69 defence-suppression missiles internally, plus 12–14 AGM-86Bs externally, or 84 500-lb (227-kg) Mk 82 bombs internally, plus 44 externally, or 24 free-falling B-61 nuclear bombs, plus 14 externally.
Status: First contract placed 20 January 1982 in programme entailing manufacture of 100 B-1Bs, the first having flown on 18 October 1984, and deliveries having commenced June 1985. Fifteenth B-1B to be delivered mid-1986, with production attaining four monthly by late 1986 and 100th delivered by April 1988.
Notes: The B-1B is a derivative of the Mach 2·2 B-1, first of four prototypes of which flew 23 December 1974. A 347-flight, 1,895-hour test programme was completed with these aircraft on 30 April 1981. The B-1B has a reduced speed capability by comparison with the B-1, being optimised for low-level penetration. After modification to incorporate many of the B-1B features, the second B-1 prototype resumed flight testing on 23 March 1983, and was joined in July 1984 by the fourth B-1 prototype which incorporated the remainder of the B-1B features. Initial operational capability is expected to be attained in 1986.

ROCKWELL B-1B

Dimensions: Span (15 deg), 136 ft 8½ in (41,67 m), (67·5 deg), 78 ft 2½ in (23,84 m); length, 146 ft 8 in (44,70 m); height, 33 ft 7¼ in (10,24 m); wing area (approx), 1,950 sq ft (181,2 m²).

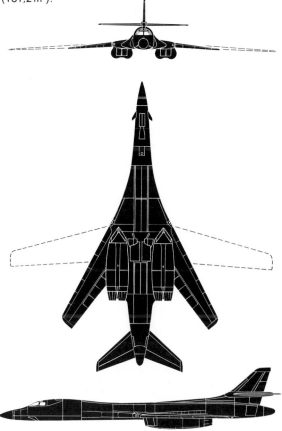

SAAB (JA) 37 VIGGEN

Country of Origin: Sweden.

Type: Single-seat air defence fighter.

Power Plant: One 16,200 lb st (7 350 kgp) dry and 28,110 lb st (12 750 kgp) reheat Volvo Flygmotor RM 8B turbofan.

Performance: Max speed (with two Rb 24 and two Rb 72 AAMs), 838 mph (1 350 km/h) or Mach=1·1 at sea level, 1,255–1,365 mph (2 020–2 195 km/h) or Mach=1·9–2·1 at 36,090 ft (11 000 m); time to 32,810 ft (10 000 m), 1·4 min; tactical radius (intercept mission), 250 mls (400 km).

Weights: Empty (approx), 26,895 lb (12 200 kg); normal loaded (four AAMs), 37,040 lb (16 800 kg); max take-off, 49,600 lb (22 500 kg).

Armament: One 30-mm Oerlikon KCA cannon, two Rb 72 Sky Flash and two (or four) Rb 24 (AIM-9L) Sidewinder AAMs. Secondary interdiction role with up to 13,227 lb (6 000 kg) of ordnance.

Status: First of four JA 37 prototypes flown June 1974, with production prototype following on 15 December 1975. First production JA 37 flown 4 November 1977, with 100th delivered on 20 August 1985 against total orders for 149 (of 329 Viggens of all types) from the Swedish Air Force.

Notes: The JA 37 is an optimised air defence version of the basic AJ 37 attack aircraft and is intended to equip eight squadrons of the Swedish Air Force. Production has been completed of the AJ 37 attack, SF 37 and SH 37 reconnaissance, and SK 37 conversion training versions, and the JA 37 manufacturing programme is expected to be completed 1987.

SAAB (JA) 37 VIGGEN

Dimensions: Span, 34 ft 9¼ in (10,60 m); length (excluding probe), 50 ft 8¼ in (15,45 m); height, 19 ft 4¼ in (5,90 m); wing area (including foreplanes), 561·88 sq ft (52,20 m²).

SAAB SF340

Country of Origin: Sweden.

Type: Regional commercial and corporate transport.

Power Plant: Two 1,735 shp General Electric CT7-5A-2 or (corporate version) 1,600 shp CT7-7E turboprops.

Performance: Max cruising speed, 320 mph (515 km/h) at 15,000 ft (4 570 m); econ cruise, 300 mph (484 km/h) at 25,000 ft (7 620 m); max initial climb, 1,765 ft/min (8,94 m/sec); range (max payload), 904 mls (1 455 km), (max fuel), 2,470 mls (3 975 km).

Weights: Operational empty (typical), 17,215 lb (7 810 kg); max take-off, 27,275 lb (12 370 kg).

Accommodation: Flight crew of two and standard regional airliner arrangement for 35 passengers three abreast with off-set aisle. Standard corporate transport arrangement provides for 16 passengers and various options are available.

Status: First of three prototypes flown 25 January 1983, followed by first production aircraft on 5 March 1984. Certification obtained on 30 May 1984, with scheduled operations (by Crossair) commencing 15 June 1984. Orders for 85 aircraft placed by beginning of December 1985 by 11 airlines and three corporate customers, with some 35 delivered.

Notes: Originally developed jointly by Saab-Scania (Sweden) and Fairchild (USA) with latter relinquishing partnership and becoming a sub-contractor on 1 November 1985. Fairchild is responsible for manufacture of the wings, engine nacelles and tail surfaces up to and including the 108th aircraft after which Saab-Scania will assume responsibility for production of the entire aircraft.

SAAB SF340

Dimensions: Span, 70 ft 4 in (21,44 m); length, 64 ft 9 in (19,72 m); height, 22 ft 6 in (6,87 m); wing area, 450 sq ft (41,81 m²).

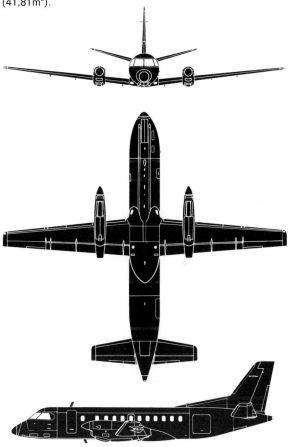

SHANSI YUN-8 (CUB)

Country of Origin: China (Soviet Union).
Type: Medium/long-range military and commercial freight transport.
Power Plant: Four 4,250 ehp Shanghai Wojiang-6 turbo-props.
Performance: Max speed, 404 mph (650 km/h) at 22,965 ft (7 000 m); max cruise, 321 mph (516 km/h) at 26,250 ft (8 000 m); max initial climb, 1,968 ft/min (10 m/sec); service ceiling, 33,465 ft (10 200 m); range (with max fuel), 3,395 mls (5 463 km).
Weights: Empty equipped, 78,265 lb (35 500 kg); max take-off, 134,480 lb (61 000 kg).
Accommodation: Normal flight crew of five, the Yun-8 has a max payload of 44,090 lb (20 000 kg) and can accommodate wheeled or tracked vehicles. Up to 100 paratroops may be carried.
Status: The Yun-8 (based on the Antonov An-12) entered production at the Shansi Transport Aircraft Plant, Hanzhong, in 1980, and is currently being manufactured for both the state airline, CAAC, and the Air Force, 17 having been delivered by mid-1985.
Notes: The Yun-8 is essentially a copy of the Antonov An-12, production of which terminated in the Soviet Union in the late 'seventies. The first Yun-8 was delivered in 1983, the military version (illustrated on the opposite page) differing from the commercial version (illustrated above) in having an extended glazed nose, the tail gun position accommodating two 23-mm cannon. A maritime surveillance derivative with western search and surveillance radar entered test mid-1985, for the monitoring of maritime pollution and for operations in connection with the fishing and offshore oil industries.

SHANSI YUN-8 (CUB)

Dimensions: Span, 124 ft 8 in (38,00 m); length, 111 ft 7½ in (34,02 m); height, 36 ft 7½ in (11,16 m); wing area, 1,311·7 sq ft (121·86 m²).

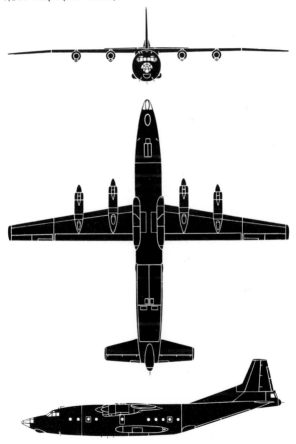

SHENYANG JIAN-8 (FINBACK)

Country of Origin: China.

Type: Single-seat Interceptor fighter.

Power Plant: Two 9,700 lb st (4 400 kgp) dry and 13,450 lb st (6 100 kgp) reheat Chengdu Wopen-7B turbojets.

Performance: (Estimated) Max speed, 1,518 mph (2 443 km/h) or Mach = 2·3 above 36,000 ft (10 975 m), 800 mph (1 287 km/h) or Mach = 1·5 at 1,000 ft (3 05 m); max initial climb (half fuel and two AAMs), 50,000 ft/min (254 m/sec); tactical radius (combat air patrol on internal fuel), 300 mls (485 km).

Weights: (Estimated) Max take-off weight, 33,070 lb (15 000 kg).

Armament: The Jian-8 display five hardpoints, two in each wing and one beneath the fuselage, and armament may be assumed to comprise four air-to-air missiles.

Status: The Jian-8 is known to have been under development since the 'sixties, but its present status is uncertain. It is not believed to have yet been manufactured on a large-scale owing to the non-availability of an adequate engine, but it participated in a flypast on 1 October 1984 to celebrate the anniversary of the foundation of the People's Republic of China and is therefore probably at least in limited service.

Notes: The Jian-8 is fundamentally a scaled-up derivative of the Jian-7, a copy of the MiG-21F, which continues in production in China and has been exported as the F-7. Conceptually, the Jian-8 is essentially similar to the experimental Mikoyan Ye-152A which appeared in 1961, and is optimised for the air superiority role. It is reported that several western companies have been consulted concerning an advanced weapon system for this fighter, suggesting that development of the Jian-8 is continuing. Unofficial reports have suggested that between 150 and 200 are now in service with the Air Force of the People's Liberation Army.

SHENYANG JIAN-8 (FINBACK)

Dimensions: (Estimated) Span, 29 ft 6 in (9,00 m); length (excluding probe), 59 ft 8½ in (18,20 m); height, 13 ft 9 in (4,20 m); wing area, 300 sq ft (28,00 m²).

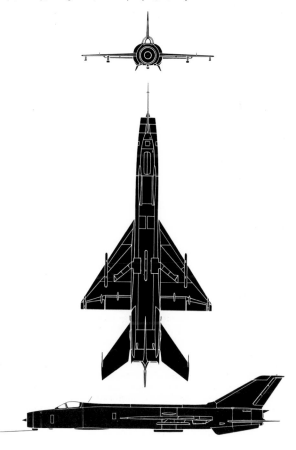

SHORTS 360

Country of Origin: United Kingdom.

Type: Regional commercial transport.

Power Plant: Two 1,327 shp Pratt & Whitney Canada PT6A-65R turboprops.

Performance: Max cruising speed, 244 mph (393 km/h) at 10,000 ft (3 050 m); long-range cruise, 201 mph (324 km/h) at 10,000 ft (3 050 m); range (with max payload), 501 mls (806 km), (with max fuel), 1,055 mls (1 697 km).

Weights: Operational empty (passenger), 16,900 lb (7 666 kg), (cargo), 15,835 lb (7 183 kg); max take-off, 26,000 lb (11 794 kg).

Accommodation: Flight crew of two with standard cabin arrangement for 36 passengers three abreast with offset aisle and provision for one cabin attendant.

Status: Prototype flown on 1 June 1981, with certification following on 3 September 1982. First production aircraft flown on 19 August 1982, entering service (with Suburban Airlines) in the following December. Orders and options totalled 120 aircraft at the beginning of November 1985 of which 77 were in service.

Notes: A growth version of the Shorts 330 (see 1983 edition), the Shorts 360 differs from its progenitor primarily in having a 3-ft (91-cm) cabin stretch ahead of the wing and an entirely redesigned rear fuselage and tail assembly. The fuselage stretch permitted the insertion of two additional three-seat rows in the main cabin, and the reduced aerodynamic drag by comparison with the earlier aircraft contributed to a higher performance. Like the Shorts 330, the Shorts 360 is unpressurised and is claimed to offer more baggage space per passenger than any comparable regional airliner.

SHORTS 360

Dimensions: Span, 74 ft 10 in (22,81 m); length, 70 ft 10 in (21,59 m); height, 23 ft 8 in (7,21 m); wing area, 454 sq ft (42,18 m²).

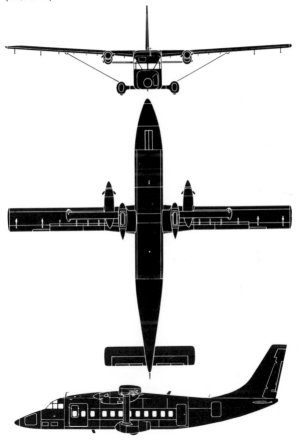

SIAI MARCHETTI S.211

Country of Origin: Italy.

Type: Tandem two-seat basic trainer.

Power Plant: One 2,500 lb st (1 134 kgp) Pratt & Whitney Canada JT15D-4C turbofan.

Performance: Max speed, 420 mph (676 km/h) at 25,000 ft (7 620 m); max cruise, 414 mph (667 km/h) at 25,000 ft (7 620 m); max initial climb, 4,200 ft/min (21,34 m/sec); service ceiling, 40,000 ft (12 190 m); max range (internal fuel with 30 min reserves), 1,036 mls (1 668 km); ferry range (with two 77 Imp gal/350 l external tanks), 1,543 mls (2 483 km).

Weights: Empty equipped, 3,560 lb (1 615 kg); max take-off (clean), 5,842 lb (2 650 kg), (with external stores), 6,834 lb (3 100 kg).

Armament: (Light attack) max external load of 1,320 lb (600 kg) distributed between four wing hardpoints.

Status: First of three prototypes flown on 10 April 1981, and first production example (for Singapore) flown on 4 October 1984, with deliveries commencing early 1985. Thirty ordered by Singapore of which first six built in Italy, disassembled and then reassembled in Singapore, next four supplied as complete kits and remaining 20 being supplied as partial kits for completion by Singapore Aerospace Manufacturing. Four ordered by Haiti.

Notes: New navigational trainer and light attack version of the S.211 scheduled to enter flight test late 1986. This will feature a more advanced cockpit including a head-up display, and consideration is being given to the installation of the 2,900 lb st (1 315 kgp) JT15D-5 engine. Features of the S.211 design include a very low airframe weight for a pure jet aircraft which compares closely with the airframe weights of contemporary turboprop-powered basic trainers.

SIAI MARCHETTI S.211

Dimensions: Span, 27 ft 8 in (8,43 m); length, 31 ft 2½ in (9,50 m); height, 12 ft 5½ in (3,80 m); wing area, 135·63 sq ft (12,60 m²).

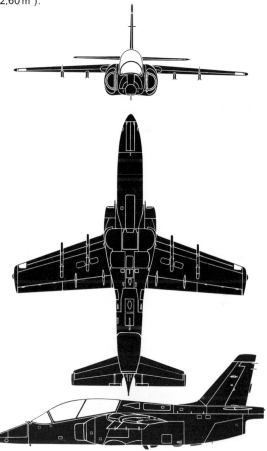

SOKO (CNAIR IAR-93B) ORAO 2

Countries of Origin: Yugoslavia and Romania.
Type: Single-seat close air support fighter.
Power Plant: Two 3,880 lb st (1 760 kgp) dry and 5,000 lb st (2 268 kgp) reheat Orao- (or Turbomecanica-) built Rolls-Royce Viper 633-41 turbojets.
Performance: Max speed (at 18,629 lb/8 450 kg), 721 mph (1 160 km/h) of Mach = 0·946 at sea level, 634 mph (1 020 km/h) at 36,090 ft (11 000 m) or Mach = 0·96; max cruise, 449 mph (723 km/h) at 22,965 ft (7 000 m); max initial climb, 13,780 ft/min (70 m/sec); service ceiling, 44,300 ft (13 500 m); tactical radius (LO-LO-LO with four rocket pods), 162 mls (260 km), (LO-LO-HI with one 110 Imp gal/500 l drop tank and four 550-lb/250-kg bombs), 280 mls (450 km) with five min loiter.
Weights: Empty equipped, 12,676 lb (5 750 kg); basic operational, 18,629 lb (8 450 kg); max take-off, 24,800 lb (11 250 kg).
Armament: Two 23-mm twin-barrel GSh-23L cannon and max external ordnance load of 3,615 lb (1 640 kg) distributed between one fuselage and four wing stations.
Status: Two prototypes flown 31 October 1974 (one in Yugoslavia and one in Romania) of Orao 1 (IAR-93A), with prototypes of the Orao 2 (IAR-93B) following during last quarter of 1983, the latter being the production version. Sixteen pre-production Orao 2/IAR-93B aircraft have been built in each country, and full-scale production is expected to commence during the course of 1986.
Notes: The Orao (Eagle) has been developed as a joint programme between SOKO in Yugoslavia and CNIAR in Romania, with final assembly lines in both countries. The Orao 1 (IAR-93A) differs primarily in having unreheated engines.

SOKO (CNIAR IAR-93B) ORAO 2

Dimensions: Span, 31 ft 6¾ in (9,62 m); length (excluding probe), 48 ft 10⅔ in (14,90 m); height, 14 ft 9⅛ in (4,50 m); wing area, 279·87 sq ft (26,00 m²).

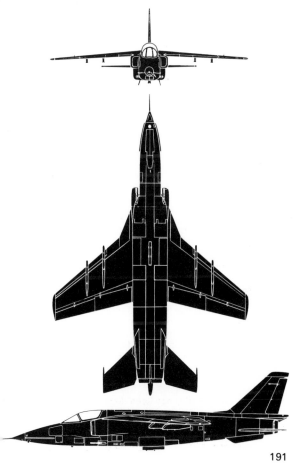

SOKO GALEB 4 (SUPER GALEB)

Country of Origin: Yugoslavia.
Type: Tandem two-seat basic and advanced trainer and light strike aricraft.
Power Plant: One 4,000 lb st (1 814 kgp) Rolls-Royce Viper 632-48 turbojet.
Performance: (At 10,494 lb/4 760 kg) Max speed, 565 mph (910 km/h) at 19,685 ft (6 000 m); max climb, 5,905 ft/min (30 m/sec); time to 26,245 ft (8 000 m), 6·0 min; combat radius (at 11,442 lb/5 190 kg) with ventral gun pack and two rocket pods, 186 mls (300 km) LO-LO-LO.
Weights: Empty equipped, 7,165 lb (3 250 kg); normal loaded (training mission), 10,494 lb (4 760 kg), (combat mission), 13,470 lb (6 110 kg); max overload, 13,955 lb (6 330 kg).
Armament: One 23-mm twin-barrel GSh-23L cannon in ventral pack and various external ordnance loads on four external hardpoints of 772 lb (350 kg) capacity inboard and 551 lb (250 kg) outboard.
Status: First of two prototypes flown on 17 July 1978 with second following on 18 December 1979. First of pre-series batch flown on 17 December 1980, with series production version entering Yugoslav Air Force service early 1983.
Notes: The G-4 Super Galeb (Super Gull) has been developed as a successor in Yugoslav Air Force service to the G-2A Galeb, but possessing no commonality with its predecessor other than design origin. Pre-series aircraft differed from the production model illustrated in having a conventional tail with neither dihedral nor anhedral, this being supplanted by an all-flying anhedralled tail. At the beginning of 1986, reheated and single-seat strike variants were being studied.

SOKO GALEB 4 (SUPER GALEB)

Dimensions: Span, 32 ft 5 in (9,88 m); length, 38 ft 11 in (11,86 m); height, 14 ft 0 in (4,28 m); wing area, 209·9 sq ft (19,50 m²).

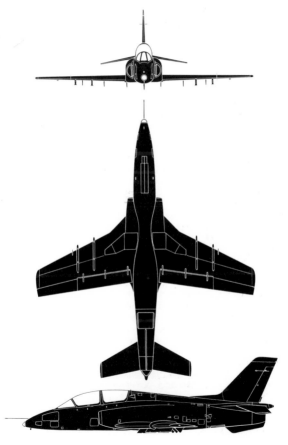

SUKHOI SU-17 (FITTER)

Country of Origin: USSR.

Type: Single-seat counterair and attack aircraft.

Power Plant: One (Fitter-H) 17,195 lb st (7 800 kgp) dry and 24,700 lb st (11 200 kgp) reheat Lyulka AL-21F or (Fitter-J) 17,635 lb st (8 000 kgp) dry and 25,350 lb st (11 500 kgp) reheat Tumansky R-29B turbojet.

Performance: (Fitter-J) Max speed (clean aircraft with 60% fuel), 1,380 mph (2 220 km/h) at 39,370 ft (12 000 m) or Mach = 2·09, 808 mph (1 300 km/h) at sea level or Mach = 1·06; max initial climb, 44,290 ft/min (225 m/sec); combat radius (with 6,614-lb/3 000-kg warload and two 176 Imp gal/800 l drop tanks), 435 mls (700 km) HI-LO-HI, 290 mls (465 km) LO-LO-LO.

Weights: Empty equipped, 21,715 lb (9 850 kg); max loaded (estimated), 39,022 lb (17 700 kg).

Armament: Two 30-mm NR-30 cannon and max external ordnance load of 6,614 lb (3 000 kg) distributed between 10 (four fuselage and six wing) hardpoints.

Status: A derivative of the fixed-geometry Su-7B, the Su-17 flew in prototype form (Fitter-B) on 2 August 1966 (as the S-221), the first series version (Fitter-C) entering service in 1971. This and subsequent Lyulka-engined versions have been exported under the designation Su-20 and Tumansky-engined versions as the Su-22, all variants supplied to the Soviet Air Forces retaining the designation Su-17. Between 800–900 currently in Soviet service with production continuing to meet attrition and export requirements.

Notes: Principal current versions of the Su-17 are the Lyulka-engined Fitter-H and -K (Illustrated above and opposite respectively) and the Tumansky-engined Fitter-J. The Su-20 and Su-22 versions have been exported to a dozen countries, including Algeria, Angola, Egypt, Iraq, North and South Yemen, Vietnam, etc.

SUKHOI SU-17 (FITTER)

Dimensions: (Estimated) Span (28 deg sweep), 45 ft 11 in (14,000 m), (68 deg sweep), 32 ft 9½ in (10,00 m); length (including probes), 59 ft 0 in (18,00 m); height, 15 ft 5 in (4,70 m); wing area, 410 sq ft (38,00 m²).

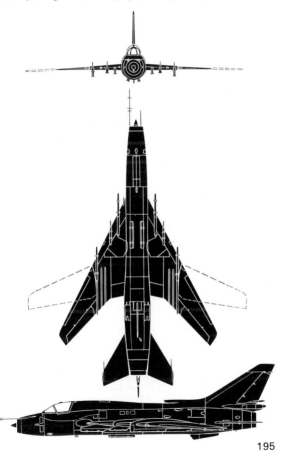

SUKHOI SU-24 (FENCER)

Country of Origin: USSR.

Type: Deep penetration interdictor and strike aircraft.

Power Plant: Two (estimated) 16,975 lb st (7 000 kgp) dry and 24,250 lb st (11 000 kgp) Lyulka or Tumansky turbojets.

Performance: (Estimated) Max speed (without external stores), 1,440 mph (2 317 km/h) above 36,000 ft (11 000 m) or Mach = 2·18, 915 mph (1 470 km/h) at sea level or Mach = 1·2; combat radius (with 4,400 lb/2 000 kg of ordnance and two jettisonable tanks), 1,115 mls (1 795 km) HI-LO-HI, 345 mls (555 km) LO-LO-LO; service ceiling, 54,135 ft (16 500 m).

Weights: (Estimated) Empty equipped, 41,890 lb (19 000 kg); max take-off, 87,000 lb (39 500 kg).

Armament: one 30-mm cannon and up to 17,635 lb (8 000 kg) of ordnance on four fuselage hardpoints (two in tandem and two side by side) and four wing hardpoints (two swivelling on the outer panels and two on fixed glove).

Status: Prototype believed flown 1970, with initial operational status achieved late 1974. Now assigned primarily to the strategic role with some 450 equipping regiments (strategic bombing and deep strike) in five air armies.

Notes: The latest variant of the Su-24 is the Fencer-C (illustrated), which, first introduced in 1981, embodies important equipment changes and different engines to those powering the earlier Fencer-A and -B versions. The Su-24 was the first Soviet aircraft in its category to carry a weapons systems officer, and has a large pulse-Doppler type radar with a scanner dish of some 50 in (1,27 m) diameter. Externally, the Fencer-C differs from earlier versions of the Su-24 primarily in the configuration of the rear fuselage box.

SUKHOI SU-24 (FENCER)

Dimensions: (Estimated) Span (16 deg sweep), 56 ft 6 in (17,25 m), (68 deg sweep), 33 ft 9 in (10,30 m); length (excluding probes), 65 ft 6 in (20,00 m); height, 18 ft 0 in (5,50 m); wing area, 452 sq ft (42,00 m²).

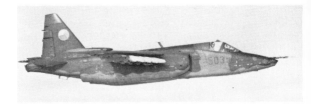

SUKHOI SU-25 (FROGFOOT)

Country of Origin: USSR.

Type: Single-seat attack and close air support aircraft.

Power Plant: Two 11,240 lb st (5 100 kgp) Tumansky R-13-300 turbojets.

Performance: (Estimated) Max speed (without external stores), 545 mph (877 km/h) at 10,000 ft (3 050 m) or Mach = 0·757; combat radius (with 8,820 lb/4 000 kg of ordnance and allowance for 30 min loiter at 5,000 ft/1 525 m), 340 mls (547 km) HI-LO-LO-HI; ferry range (with four 108 Imp gal/490 l external tanks), 1,800 mls (2 895 km).

Weights: (Estimated) Empty, 22,045 lb (10 000 kg); max take-off, 41,890–44,090 lb (19 000–20 000 kg).

Armament: One 30-mm cannon and up to 8,820 lb (4 000 kg) of ordnance on 10 wing hardpoints, including 57-mm and 80-mm unguided rockets, 1,100-lb (500-kg) retarded cluster bombs, etc. Air-to-air missiles for self defence may be carried on outboard hardpoints.

Status: The Su-25 was first observed under test in the late 'seventies, prototypes having presumably flown during 1977–78, with initial deliveries to the Soviet Air Forces following in 1980–81. The first export customer for the Su-25 was Czechoslovakia, and production was continuing at the beginning of 1986 at Tbilisi at a rate of approximately 100 aircraft annually.

Notes: The Su-25 is broadly comparable with the USAF's Fairchild A-10A Thunderbolt II. It features a levered-suspension type undercarriage with low-pressure tyres suitable for rough field operation and wingtip fairings of flattened ovoid section which incorporate split spoilers operated symmetrically or differentially to aid low-altitude manoeuvrability. The Su-25 has been deployed operationally in Afghanistan for more than three years.

SUKHOI SU-25 (FROGFOOT)

Dimensions: (Estimated) Span, 48 ft 0 in (14,63 m); length (excluding nose probes), 46 ft 10 in (14,30 m); height, 16 ft 6 in (5,00 m). Wing area, 419·8 sp ft (39,00 m²).

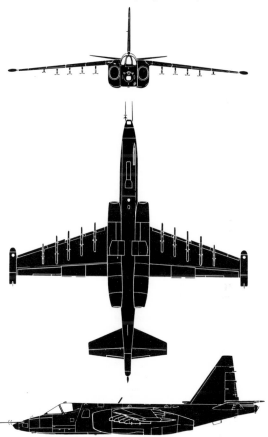

SUKHOI SU-27 (FLANKER)

Country of Origin: USSR.
Type: Single-seat multi-role fighter.
Power Plant: Two (estimated) 20,000 lb st (9 070 kgp) dry and 30,000 lb st (13 610 kgp) reheat turbofans.
Performance: (Estimated) Max speed, 1,520 mph (1 445 km/h) above 36,100 ft (11 00 m) or Mach = 2·3, 835 mph (1 345 km/h) at sea level or Mach = 1·1; initial climb, 60,000 ft/min (304,5 m/sec); tactical radius (high-altitude air-air mission with four AAMs), 715 mls (1 150 km).
Weights: (Estimated) Empty equipped, 39,000 lb (17 690 kg); loaded (air-air mission), 44,000 lb (19 960 kg); max take-off, 63,500 lb (28 805 kg).
Armament: Up to six AA-10 medium-range AAMs for air-air mission, or up to 13,200 lb (5 990 kg) of air-to-ground weapons for attack mission.
Status: First identified in 1977, the Su-27 is believed to have entered series production at Komsomolsk in 1980–81 and was reported to have achieved initial operational capability by the beginning of 1986.
Notes: Generally comparable with the F-15 Eagle and possessing a fundamentally similar configuration to that of the smaller and lighter MiG-29 Fulcrum, the Su-27 Flanker is primarily an all-weather counterair fighter possessing secondary attack capability. The Su-27 has undergone considerable redesign during development, a major change being the movement outboard of the vertical tail surfaces to extensions of the wing along the sides of the rear fuselage. Equipment includes a track-while-scan radar, a pulse-Doppler look-down/shootdown weapon system, infrared search and tracking, and a digital data link.

SUKHOI SU-27 (FLANKER)

Dimensions: (Estimated) Span, 47 ft 6 in (14,50 m); length, 60 ft 0 in (21,00 m); wing area, 538 sq ft (50,00 m²).

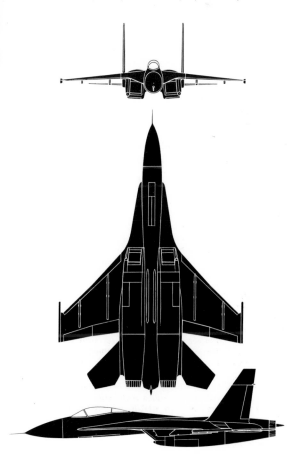

TUPOLEV TU-22M (BACKFIRE-B)

Country of Origin: USSR.

Type: Medium-range strategic bomber and maritime strike/reconnaissance aircraft.

Power Plant: Two (estimated) 33,070 lb st (15 000 kgp) dry and 46,300 lb st (21 000 kgp) reheat Kuznetsov turbofans.

Performance: (Estimated) Max speed (short-period dash), 1,265 mph (2 036 km/h) or Mach=1·91 at 39,370 ft (12 000 m), (sustained), 1,056 mph (1 700 km/h) or Mach=1·6 at 39,370 ft (12 000 m), 685 mph (1 100 km/h) or Mach=0·9 at sea level; combat radius (unrefuelled with single AS-4 ASM and high-altitude subsonic mission profile), 2,610 mls (4 200 km); max unrefuelled combat range (with 12,345 lb/5 600 kg internal ordnance), 3,420 mls (5 500 km).

Weights: (Estimated) Max take-off, 260,000 lb (118 000 kg).

Armament: Remotely-controlled tail barbette housing twin 23-mm NR-23 cannon. Internal load of free-falling weapons up to 12,345 lb (5 600 kg) or one AS-4 Kitchen inertially-guided stand-off missile housed semi-externally.

Status: Flight testing of initial prototype commenced late 1969, with pre-production series of up to 12 aircraft following in 1972–73. Initial version (Backfire-A) was built in small numbers only. Initial operational capability attained with Backfire-B in 1975–76, production rate of 30 annually being attained in 1977 and remaining constant at beginning of 1986, when 175–180 were in service with Soviet Long-range Aviation and a similar quantity with the Soviet Naval Air Force. An advanced version, the Backfire-C, with redesigned engine air intakes and presumably uprated engines has been reported under test, but its production status was uncertain at the beginning of 1986.

TUPOLEV TU-22M (BACKFIRE-B)

Dimensions: (Estimated) Span (20 deg sweep), 115 ft 0 in (35,00 m), (55 deg sweep), 92 ft 0 in (28,00 m); length, 138 ft 0 in (42,00 m); height, 29 ft 6 in (9,00 m); wing area, 1,830 sq ft (170,00 m²).

TUPOLEV (BLACKJACK-A)

Country of Origin: USSR.

Type: Long-range strategic bomber and maritime strike/reconnaissance aircraft.

Power Plant: Four 30,000 lb st (13 610 kgp) dry and 50,000 lb st (22 680 kgp) reheat turbofan.

Performance: (Estimated) Max (over-target dash) speed, 1,380 mph (2 220 km/h) at 40,000 ft (12 200 m), or Mach = 2·09; range cruise, 595 mph (960 km/h) at 45,000 ft (13 720 m), or Mach = 0·9; unrefuelled combat radius, 4,540 mls (7 300 km).

Weights: (Estimated) Empty, 260,000 lb (117 950 kg); max take-off, 590,000 lb (267 625 kg).

Armament: Maximum weapon load (estimated), of 36,000 lb (16 330 kg).

Status: First identified under test (at Ramenskoye) in 1979. Believed to have entered production 1982–83, with initial operational capability anticipated in 1986–7.

Notes: Initially known by the provisional identification designation Ram-P and a product of the Tupolev design bureau, Blackjack-A is apparently some 25 per cent larger than the Rockwell B-1B and is intended as a replacement for the intercontinental attack version of the Tu-95 Bear. It is anticipated that the Soviet Union will build a series of about 100.

TUPOLEV (BLACKJACK-A)

Dimensions: (Estimated) Span (minimum sweep), 150 ft 0 in (54,00 m), (maximum sweep), 101 ft 0 in (30,75 m); length, 175 ft 0 in (53,35 m); wing area, 2,500 sq ft (232,25 m²).

TUPOLEV TU-154M (CARELESS)

Country of Origin: USSR.
Type: Medium haul commercial transport.
Power Plant: Three 23,380 lb st (10 605 kgp) Soloviev D-30KU-154-III turbofans.
Performance: Max cruising speed, 603 mph (970 km/h) at 39,370 ft (12 000 m); econ cruise, 528 mph (850 km/h) at 29,500–42,650 ft (9 000–13 000 m); range (with max payload), 2,420 mls (3 900 km), (with 26,455-lb/12 000-kg payload), 3,230 mls (5 200 km).
Weights: Empty, 119,050 lb (54 000 kg); max take-off, 220,460 lb (100 000 kg).
Accommodation: Flight crew of four and basic arrangement for 169 passengers six abreast with optional arrangements for 180 economy class passengers or 162 passengers in a mix of first, tourist and economy class seating.
Status: The Tu-154M prototype entered flight test mid-1982, with initial customer deliveries (to Aeroflot) following from December 1984. The first of six prototype and pre-series examples of the original Tu-154 flew on 4 October 1968.
Notes: The Tu-154M is fundamentally a re-engined and modernised (revised navigation system with triplex INS, redesigned tailplane, revised slats and spoilers, etc) Tu-154B-2 which was, in turn, an improved version of the Tu-154B introduced in 1977. The Tu-154M has been ordered by CAAC, Cubana, LOT and Syrianair.

TUPOLEV TU-154M (CARELESS)

Dimensions: Span, 123 ft 2½ in (37,55 m); length, 157 ft 1¾ in (47,90 m); height, 37 ft 4¾ in (11,40 m); wing area, 2,169 sq ft (201·45 m²).

UTVA LASTA

Country of Origin: Yugoslavia.

Type: Tandem two-seat primary/basic trainer.

Power Plant: One 300 hp Avco Lycoming AEIO-540-L1B5-D six-cylinder horizontally-opposed engine.

Performance: (Estimated) Max speed, 214 mph (345 km/h) at sea level; max initial climb, 1,772 ft/min (9,0 m/sec).

Weights: Empty equipped, 2,337 lb (1 060 kg); max take-off, 3,593 lb (1 630 kg).

Armament: (Weapons training and light strike) Two universal ordnance pods with a total weight of 529 lb (240 kg), two 16-tube 57-mm rocket pods or two twin 7,62-mm machine gun pods.

Status: The first of two prototypes of the Lasta entered flight test summer of 1945, at which time work had begun on a pre-series of 10 aircraft.

Notes: The Lasta (Swallow) has been designed by the Air Force Technical Institute at Žarkovo and is being manufactured by the UTVA concern at Pančevo for the Yugoslav Air Force as a successor to the UTVA-75. In the same category as the TB 30 Epsilon and the T-35 Pillán, the Lasta is expected to enter service from late 1986 when an initial course will be inaugurated on the pre-series aircraft. The cockpits of the Lasta are based on those of the Galeb 4 basic/advanced trainer.

UTVA LASTA

Dimensions: Span, 27 ft 4⅓ in (8,34 m); length, 26 ft 4½ in (8,04 m); height, 14 ft 7¼ in (4,45 m); wing area, 118·4 sq ft (11,00 m²).

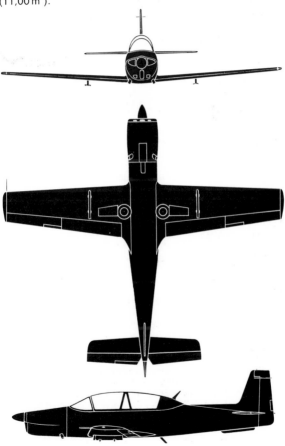

VALMET L-80 TP

Country of Origin: Finland.
Type: Side-by-side two-seat primary/basic trainer.
Power Plant: One 360 shp Allison 250-B17D turboprop.
Performance: Max speed, 211 mph (340 km/h) at 9,840 ft (3 000 m); max initial climb, 1,968 ft/min (10 m/sec); time to 9,840 ft (3 000 m), 5·5 min; range (with 30 min reserves), 808 mls (1 300 km).
Weights: Empty equipped, 1,962 lb (890 kg); max take-off, 4,189 lb (1 900 kg).
Armament: (Weapons training and light strike) Max external load of 1,764 lb (800 kg) distributed between six wing hard-points, typical loads as a single-seater including four 330·5-lb (150-kg) bombs or two 551-lb (250-kg) bombs, plus two flare pods.
Status: First prototype flown on 12 February 1985, with second scheduled to enter flight test in May 1986.
Notes: The L-80 TP, developed by the Defence Equipment Group of Valmet, is one of the lightest of current turboprop-powered training aircraft and is in a broadly similar category to the Siai Marchetti SF.260TP and such projected types as the ENAER Turbo Pillán. The first and second prototypes utilise an all-aluminium wing, but the proposed third prototype will have a Valmet-developed all-composite wing based on the same aerofoil, this being offered as a customer option. Designed to provide instruction from *ab initio* to advanced jet conversion, the L-80 TP is claimed to offer a lower total system cost than most current training aircraft of comparable performance.

VALMET L-80 TP

Dimensions: Span, 33 ft 3⅔ in (10,15 m); length, 25 ft 11 in (7,90 m); height, 9 ft 4¼ in (2,85 m); wing area, 158·77 sq ft (14,75 m²).

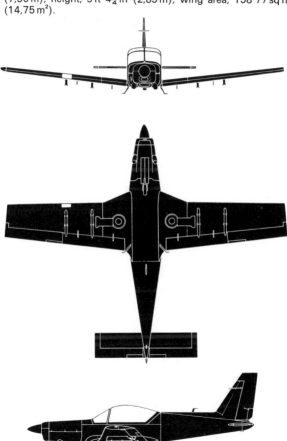

YAKOVLEV YAK-38 (FORGER-A)

Country of Origin: USSR.

Type: Single-seat shipboard air defence and strike fighter.

Power Plant: One 17,985 lb st (8 160 kgp) Lyulka AL-21 lift/cruise turbojet and two tandem-mounted 7,875 lb st (3 570 kgp) Kolesov lift turbojets.

Performance: (Estimated) Max speed, 648 mph (1 042 km/h) or Mach=0·85 at sea level, 627 mph (1 010 km/h) or Mach=0·95 above 36,000 ft (10 970 m); max initial climb, 14,750 ft/min (74,93 m/sec); service ceiling, 39,375 ft (12 000 m); combat radius with max ordnance, 150 mls (240 km) LO-LO-LO, 230 mls (370 km) HI-LO-HI, (air defence with two GSh-23 gun pods and two drop tanks), 115 mls (185 km) with 1 hr 15 min on station.

Weights: (Estimated) Empty equipped 16,500 lb (7 485 kg); max take-off, 25,794 lb (11 700 kg).

Armament: (Air Defence) Two AA-8 Aphid AAMs or two podded 23-mm twin-barrel GSh-23 cannon, or (strike) up to 7,936 lb (3 600 kg) of bombs, air-to-surface missiles such as AS-7 Kerry and drop tanks.

Status: Believed to have flown as a prototype in 1971, and initially referred to as the Yak-36MP, the Yak-38 is deployed aboard the carriers *Kiev*, *Minsk*, *Novorossisk* and *Kharkov*, each vessel having a complement of 12 fighters of this type.

Notes: The Yak-38 is capable of rolling vertical take-offs as distinct from orthodox short take-offs which benefit from wing-induced lift, such RVTOs not usually exceeding 35 mph (56 km/h) and presumably being intended to avoid over-heating the deck plates. Primary operational tasks are fleet air defence against shadowing maritime surveillance aircraft, reconnaissance and anti-ship strike.

YAKOVLEV YAK-38 (FORGER-A)

Dimensions: (Estimated) Span, 24 ft 7 in (7,50 m); length, 52 ft 6 in (16,00 m); height, 11 ft 0 in (3,35 m); wing area, 199·14 sq ft (18,50 m²).

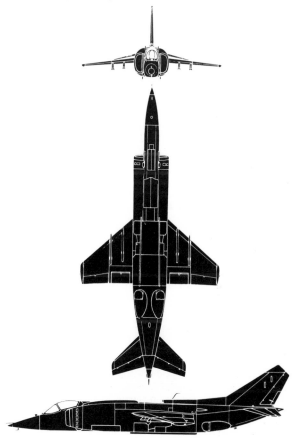

YAKOVLEV YAK-42 (CLOBBER)

Country of Origin: USSR.

Type: Medium-range commercial transport.

Power Plant: Three 14,330 lb st (6 500 kgp) Lotarev D-36 turbofans.

Performance: Max cruising speed, 503 mph (810 km/h at 25,000 ft (7 620 m); econ cruise, 466 mph (750 km/h) at 25,000 ft (7 620 m); range (with max payload), 559 mls (900 km), (with 23,150-lb/10 500-kg payload), 1,242 mls (2 000 km), (with 14,330-lb/6 500-kg payload), 1,864 mls (3 000 km).

Weights: Empty, 63,845 lb (28 960 kg); max take-off, 117,950 lb (53 500 kg).

Accommodation: Crew of two on flight deck and single-class cabin with 120 seats six abreast with central aisle.

Status: First of three prototypes flown on 7 March 1975, and production of initial series of 200 initiated at Smolensk in 1978, with 10 flown by mid-1981. Withdrawn from service for unspecified reason in 1982, but restored to Aeroflot routes in 1984, when production was resumed.

Notes: At the beginning of 1986, development was in process of a "stretched" version of the basic design designated Yak-42M. This features a 14 ft 9 in (4,50 m) longer fuselage to accommodate 156–168 passengers, max take-off weight being increased to 145,000 lb (66 000 kg). The engines of the Yak-42M are 16,550 lb st (7 500 kgp) Lotarev D-436 turbofans and payload over a 1,550-mile (2 500-km) range is claimed to be 35,275 lb (16 000 kg). The Yak-42 programme has suffered a number of delays resulting from unspecified causes, but production for Aeroflot is now taking place.

YAKOVLEV YAK-42 (CLOBBER)

Dimensions: Span, 112 ft 2½ in (34,20 m); length, 119 ft 4¼ in (36,38 m); height, 32 ft 1¾ in (9,80 m); wing area, 1,615 sq ft (150,00 m²).

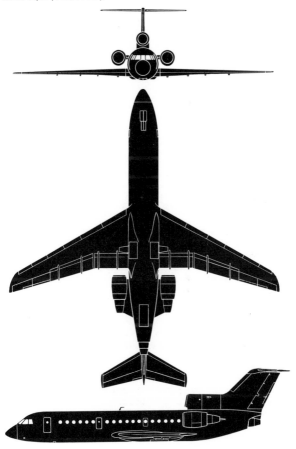

AEROSPATIALE AS 332L SUPER PUMA

Country of Origin: France.
Type: Medium transport helicopter.
Power Plant: Two 1,755 shp Turboméca Makila turboshafts.
Performance: (At 18,080 lb/8 200 kg) Max speed, 184 mph (296 km/h); max cruise, 173 mph (278 km/h) at sea level; max inclined climb. 1,810 ft/min (9,2 m/sec); hovering ceiling (in ground effect), 9,840 ft (3 000 m), (out of ground effect), 7,545 ft (2 300 m); range, 527 mls (850 km).
Weights: Empty, 9,635 lb (4 370 kg); normal loaded, 18,080 lb (8 200 kg); max take-off, 19,840 lb (9 000 kg).
Dimensions: Rotor diam, 49 ft 5¾ in (15,08 m); fuselage length, 48 ft 7¾ in (14,82 m).
Notes: First flown on 10 October 1980, the AS 332L is a stretched (by 2·5 ft/76 cm) version of the basic Super Puma which is being produced in civil (AS 332C) and military (AS 332B) versions. The AS 332L and M (illustrated) are respectively civil and military variants of the stretched model, and the AS 332F is a navalised ASW version with an overall length of 42 ft 1⅓ in (12,83 m) with rotor blades folded. Deliveries of the AS 332C began in October 1981 with the AS 332L following in December. One hundred and sixty Super Pumas (all versions) delivered by beginning of 1986, when production was four monthly and some 250 had been ordered. The AS 332B and C carry 20 troops and 17 passengers respectively. Eleven AS 332s have been assembled by Nurtanio in Indonesia and the Super Puma is now being built as the NAS-332, the first two being delivered on 29 December 1984.

AEROSPATIALE AS 350 ECUREUIL

Country of Origin: France.

Type: Six-seat light general-purpose utility helicopter.

Power Plant: (AS 350B) One 641 shp Turboméca Arriel, or (AS 350D) 615 shp Avco Lycoming LTS 101-600A2 turboshaft.

Performance: (AS 350B) Max speed, 169 mph (272 km/h) at sea level; cruise, 144 mph (232 km/h); max inclined climb, 1,555 ft/min (7,9 m/sec); hovering ceiling (in ground effect), 9,678 ft (2 950 m), (out of ground effect), 7,382 ft (2 250 m); range, 435 mls (700 km) at sea level.

Weights: Empty, 2,348 lb (1 065 kg); max take-off, 4,630 lb (2 100 kg).

Dimensions: Rotor diam, 35 ft 0¾ in (10,69 m); fuselage length (tail rotor included), 35 ft 9½ in (10,91 m).

Notes: The first Ecureuil (Squirrel) was flown on 27 June 1974 (with an LTS 101 turboshaft) and the second on 14 February 1975 (with an Arriel). The LTS 101-powered version (AS 350D) is being marketed in the USA as the AStar. By the beginning of 1986, production rate of both versions combined was running at 10 monthly, with some 800 delivered and more than 1,000 ordered. The standard Ecureuil is a six-seater and features include composite rotor blades, a so-called Star-flex rotor head, simplified dynamic machinery and modular assemblies to simplify changes in the field. The AS 350D AStar version is assembled and finished by Aérospatiale Helicopter at Grand Prairie, Alberta. Ecureuils are being assembled in Brazil as the HB 350B Esquilo.

AEROSPATIALE AS 355F ECUREUIL 2

Country of Origin: France.
Type: Six-seat light general-purpose utility helicopter.
Power Plant: Two 420 shp Allison 250-C20F turboshafts.
Performance: Max speed, 169 mph (272 km/h) at sea level; max. cruise, 144 mph (232 km/h) at sea level; max inclined climb, 1,614 ft/min (8,2 m/sec); hovering ceiling (out of ground effect), 7,900 ft (2 410 m); service ceiling, 14,800 ft (4 510 m); range, 470 mls (756 km) at sea level.
Weights: Empty, 2,778 lb (1 260 kg); max take-off, 5,292 lb (2 400 kg).
Dimensions: Rotor diam, 35 ft 0¾ in (10,69 m); fuselage length (tail rotor included), 35 ft 9½ in (10,91 m).
Notes: Flown for the first time on 27 September 1979, the Ecureuil 2 employs an essentially similar airframe and similar dynamic components to those of the single-engined AS 350 Ecureuil (see page 217), and is intended primarily for the North American market on which it is known as the TwinStar. Deliveries of the Ecureuil 2/TwinStar commenced in July 1981. From the first quarter of 1982, the production model has been the AS 355F which has higher max take-off weight than the AS 355E that it has succeeded. The AS 355F has main rotor blades of increased chord, twin-body servo command units and two electrical generators. Some 300 delivered by beginning of 1986 against orders for about 350. The AS 355M (illustrated) is an armed military model, 50 examples of which have been ordered by the *Armée de l'Air*. A TOW installation is available for the anti-armour role.

AEROSPATIALE SA 365 DAUPHIN 2

Country of Origin: France.
Type: Multi-purpose and transport helicopter.
Power Plant: Two 700 shp Turboméca Arriel 1C turboshafts.
Performance: (SA 365N) Max speed, 190 mph (305 km/h); max continuous cruise, 173 mph (278 km/h) at sea level; max inclined climb, 1,279 ft/min (6,5 m/sec); hovering ceiling (in ground effect), 3,296 ft (1 005 m), (out of ground effect), 3,116 ft (950 m); range, 548 mls (882 km) at sea level.
Weights: Empty, 4,288 lb (1 945 kg); max take-off, 8,487 lb (3 850 kg).
Dimensions: Rotor diam, 39 ft 1½ in (11,93 m); fuselage length (including tail rotor), 37 ft 6⅓ in (11,44 m).
Notes: Flown as a prototype on 31 March 1979, the SA 365 is the latest derivative of the basic Dauphin (see 1982 edition), and is being manufactured in four versions, the 10–14-seat commercial SA 365N, the military SA 365M which can transport 13 commandos and carry eight HOT missiles, the navalised SA 365F with folding rotor, Agrion radar and four AS 15TT anti-ship missiles (20 ordered by Saudi Arabia for delivery from 1984) and the SA 366G, an Avco Lycoming LTS 101-750-powered search and rescue version for the US Coast Guard as the HH-65A Seaguard. Ninety of the last version have been procured by the US Coast Guard, with completion in 1985. Production of the SA 365N was five monthly at the beginning of 1986 when about 240 had been delivered against total orders for some 350 Dauphin helicopters (all versions).

AGUSTA A 109A MK II

Country of Origin: Italy.
Type: Eight-seat light utility helicopter.
Power Plant: Two 420 shp Allison 250-C20B turboshafts.
Performance: (At 5,402 lb/2 450 kg) Max speed, 193 mph (311 km/h); max continuous cruise, 173 mph (278 km/h); range cruise, 143 mph (231 km/h); max inclined climb rate, 1,820 ft/min (9,25 m/sec); hovering ceiling (in ground effect), 9,800 ft (2 987 m), (out of ground effect), 6,800 ft (2 073 m); max range, 356 mls (573 km).
Weights: Empty equipped, 3,125 lb (1 418 kg); max take-off, 5,730 lb (2 600 kg).
Dimensions: Rotor diam, 36 ft 1 in (11,00 m); fuselage length, 35 ft 2½ in (10,73 m).
Notes: The A 109A Mk II is an improved model of the basic A 109A, the first of four prototypes of which flew on 4 August 1971, with customer deliveries commencing late 1976. Some 260 A 109As had been ordered by the beginning of 1986. The Mk II, which supplanted the initial model in production during 1981, has been the subject of numerous detail improvements, the transmission rating of the combined engines being increased from 692 to 740 shp, and the maximum continuous rating of each engine from 385 to 420 shp. An anti-armour version has been procured by Argentine, Libyan and Yugoslav forces. In 1984, a "widebody" version of the A 109 Mk II was introduced. Flown in September of that year, this has new side panels adding 8 in (20 cm) to the cabin width.

AGUSTA A 109K

Country of Origin: Italy.

Type: Light military utility helicopter.

Power Plant: Two 700 shp Turboméca Arriel 1K turboshafts.

Performance: Max speed (clean), 193 mph (311 km/h) at sea level; max cruise, 168 mph (270 km/h) at sea level; max inclined climb rate, 1,820 ft/min (9,2 m/sec); hovering ceiling (out of ground effect), 15,300 ft (4 665 m); ferry range, 460 mls (740 km).

Weights: Empty, 3,515 lb (1 595 kg); max take-off, 6,285 lb (2 850 kg).

Dimensions: Rotor diam, 36 ft 1 in (11,00 m); fuselage length, 36 ft 6 in (11,11 m).

Notes: The A 109K is a re-engined, military derivative of the A 109A Mk II (see page 220) optimised for hot and high conditions. A prototype of the A 109K was flown in April 1983, with a more representative second prototype following in March 1984. Apart from the engines, the A 109K differs from earlier models in having a fixed undercarriage and more advanced avionics. It can accommodate up to seven troops or two casualty stretchers and two medical attendants in the medevac role. Weapons may be carried on four attachment points and typically comprise four outrigger-mounted TOW or six HOT anti-armour missiles, 7,62-mm machine gun pods, or 12-tube (2,75-in/70-mm) or seven-tube (3,2-in/81-mm) rocket pods. Versions equipped for search and rescue are proposed.

AGUSTA A 129 MANGUSTA

Country of Origin: Italy.

Type: Two-seat light attack helicopter.

Power Plant: Two 915 shp Rolls-Royce Gem 2 Mk 1004D turboshafts.

Performance: (Estimated) Max speed, 173 mph (278 km/h); cruise (TOW configuration at 8,377 lb/3 800 kg), 149 mph (240 km/h) at 5,740 ft (1 750 m); max inclined climb (at 8,377 lb/3 800 kg), 2,087 ft/min (10,6 m/sec); hovering ceiling at 8,090 lb/3 670 kg), (in ground effect), 10,795 ft (3 290 m), (out of ground effect), 7,840 ft (2 390 m).

Weights: Mission, 8,080 lb (3 665 kg); max take-off, 8,377 lb (3 800 kg).

Dimensions: Rotor diam, 39 ft 0½ in (11,90 m); fuselage length, 40 ft 3¼ in (12,27 m).

Notes: The A 129 Mangusta (Mongoose) dedicated attack and anti-armour helicopter with full night/bad weather combat capability has been developed to an Italian Army requirement. The first of four flying prototypes commenced flight test on 15 September 1983, and first deliveries are scheduled for 1987, with 66 expected to be funded for the Italian Army. In typical anti-armour configuration, the A 129 will be armed with eight TOW missiles to which can be added 2·75-in (7-cm) rocket launchers for suppressive fire. The fourth prototype, flown in March 1985, has a unified electronic control system, combining flight controls, and weapon aiming and firing systems.

BELL AH-1S HUEYCOBRA

Country of Origin: USA.

Type: Two-seat light attack helicopter.

Power Plant: One 1,800 shp Avco Lycoming T53-L-703 turboshaft.

Performance: Max speed, 172 mph (277 km/h), (TOW configuration), 141 mph (227 km/h); max inclined climb, 1,620 ft/min (8,23 m/sec); hovering ceiling TOW configuration (in ground effect), 12,200 ft (3 720 m); max range, 357 mls (574 km).

Weights: (TOW configuration) Operational empty, 6,479 lb (2 939 kg); max take-off, 10,000 lb (4 535 kg).

Dimensions: Rotor diam, 44 ft 0 in (13,41 m); fuselage length, 44 ft 7 in (13,59 m).

Notes: The AH-1S is a dedicated attack and anti-armour helicopter serving primarily with the US Army which had received 297 new-production AH-1S HueyCobras by mid-1981, plus 290 resulting from the conversion of earlier AH-1G and AH-1Q HueyCobras. Current planning calls for conversion of a further 372 AH-1Gs to AH-1S standards, and both conversion and new-production AH-1S HueyCobras have been progressively upgraded to "Modernised AH-1S" standard, the entire programme having been scheduled for completion in 1985, resulting in a total of 959 "Modernised" AH-1S HueyCobras. In December 1979, one YAH-1S was flown with a four-bladed main rotor as the Model 249. The AH-1S is being licence-built in Japan by Fuji for the Ground Self-Defence Force which is to receive 54 examples.

BELL AH-1W SUPERCOBRA

Country of Origin: USA.

Type: Two-seat light attack helicopter.

Power Plant: Two 1,693 shp General Electric T700-GE-401 turboshafts.

Performance: Max cruising speed, 184 mph (296 km/h) at 3,000 ft (915 m); hovering ceiling (out of ground effect), 10,000 ft (3 050 m); range, 380 mls (611 km) at 3,000 ft (915 m).

Weights: Empty, 9,700 lb (4 400 kg); max take-off, 14,750 lb (6 691 kg).

Dimensions: Rotor diam, 48 ft 0 in (14,63 m); fuselage length, 45 ft 3 in (13,79 m).

Notes: Flown for the first time on 16 November 1983, the AH-1W SuperCobra is an enhanced-capability derivative of the AH-1T SeaCobra (see 1984 edition) of the US Marine Corps. The first of an initial batch of 22 SuperCobras is scheduled to be delivered to the USMC in March 1986, and a follow-on batch of a further 22 was ordered September 1985. More powerful and more heavily armed than the SeaCobra, the primary USMC mission of the SuperCobra will be to provide escort for troop-carrying helicopters, and in this role it can augment its 20-mm three-barrel rotary cannon with up to four AIM-9L Sidewinder missiles on the stub-wing pylons. A typical load for the anti-armour mission can comprise eight laser-guided Hellfire launch-and-leave missiles, other weapon options including 76 2·75-in (70-mm) unguided rockets, two GPU-2A 20-mm gun pods or 16 5-in (12,7-mm) Zunis.

BELL MODEL 214ST

Country of Origin: USA.
Type: Medium transport helicopter (20 seats).
Power Plant: Two 1,625 shp (limited to combined output of 2,250 shp) General Electric CT7-2A turboshafts.
Performance: Max cruising speed, 164 mph (264 km/h) at sea level, 161 mph (259 km/h) at 4,000 ft (1 220 m); hovering ceiling (in ground effect), 12,600 ft (3 840 m), (out of ground effect), 3,300 ft (1 005 m); range (standard fuel), 460 mls (740 km).
Weights: Max take-off (internal or external load), 17,500 lb (7 938 kg).
Dimensions: Rotor diam, 52 ft 0 in (15,85 m); fuselage length, 50 ft 0 in (15,24 m).
Notes: The Model 214ST (Super Transport) is a significantly improved derivative of the Model 214B BigLifter (see 1978 edition), production of which was phased out early 1981, initial customer deliveries of the Model 214ST beginning early 1982. The Model 214ST test-bed was first flown in March 1977, and the first of three representative prototypes (one in military configuration and two for commercial certification) commenced its test programme in August 1979. Work on an initial series of 100 helicopters of this type commenced in 1981. A version with wheel landing gear was certificated in March 1983, and alternative layouts are available for either 16 or 17 passengers. Military operators include the Venezuelan and Peruvian air forces, and the Royal Thai Army. An example in Chinese service is illustrated above.

BELL MODEL 222B

Country of Origin: USA.

Type: Eight/ten-seat light utility and transport helicopter.

Power Plant: Two 680 shp Avco Lycoming LTS 101-750C-1 turboshafts.

Performance: Max cruising speed, 150 mph (241 km/h) at sea level, 146 mph (235 km/h) at 8,000 ft (2 400 m); max climb, 1,730 ft/min (8,8 m/sec); hovering ceiling (in ground effect), 10,300 ft (3 135 m), (out of ground effect), 6,400 ft (1 940 m); range (no reserves), 450 mls (724 km) at 8,000 ft (2 400 m).

Weights: Empty equipped, 4,577 lb (2 076 kg); max take-off (standard configuration), 8,250 lb (3 742 kg).

Dimensions: Rotor diam, 42 ft 0 in (12,80 m); fuselage length, 39 ft 9 in (12,12 m).

Notes: The first of five prototypes of the Model 222 was flown on 13 August 1976, an initial production series of 250 helicopters of this type being initiated in 1978, with production deliveries commencing in January 1980, and some 240 delivered by beginning of 1986, when production rate was one monthly. Several versions of the Model 222 are on offer or under development, these including an executive version with a flight crew of two and five or six passengers, and the so-called "offshore" model with accommodation for eight passengers and a flight crew of two. The Model 222B has a larger main rotor and uprated power plant, a utility version, the Model 222UT, having been certificated mid 1983.

226

BELL MODEL 400 TWINRANGER

Country of Origin: USA (Canada).
Type: Multi-purpose seven-seat light helicopter.
Power Plant: Two 420 shp Allison 250-C20 turboshafts.
Performance: (Manufacturer's estimates) Max cruising speed, 161 mph (259 km/h); hovering ceiling (out of ground effect), 7,600 ft (2 315 m); max range, 450 + mls (724 + km).
Weights: Empty, 3,075 lb (1 395 kg); max take-off, 5,500 lb (2 495 kg).
Dimensions: Rotor diam, 35 ft 0 in (10,67 m).
Notes: The Model 400 TwinRanger, the first prototype of which was flown on 4 July 1984, is the first of a new family of commercial and military single- and twin-engined helicopters, this including the Model 400A with a 1,000 shp Pratt & Whitney (Canada) PW209T turboshaft and the Model 440 which will employ composites for some of its major components. This family of helicopters is being manufactured by a new Bell facility in Canada under a contract with the Canadian government, and customer deliveries are expected to commence (Model 400) in 1986. The Model 400A is due to fly in 1987, and will become available in the spring of 1989, and the Model 440 is to fly late 1988, with customer deliveries commencing in the following year. During the initial stages of the Canadian programme, the rotor heads, rotor blades, transmission systems and other complex components will be manufactured in the USA, the Canadian plant building the airframes and undertaking final assembly.

BELL MODEL 406 (OH-58D)

Country of Origin: USA.

Type: Two-seat scout helicopter.

Power Plant: One 650 shp Allison 250-C30R turboshaft.

Performance: Max speed, 147 mph (237 km/h) at 4,000 ft (1 220 m); max cruise, 138 mph (222 km/h) at 2,000 ft (610 m); max inclined climb, 1,540 ft/min (7,82 m/sec); hovering ceiling (in ground effect), 12,000+ ft (3 660+ m), (out of ground effect), 11,200 ft (3 415 m); range (no reserves), 345 mls (556 km).

Weights: (Manufacturer's estimates) Empty, 2,825 lb (1 281 kg); max take-off, 4,500 lb (2 041 kg).

Dimensions: Rotor diam, 35 ft 0 in (10,67 m); fuselage length, 33 ft 10 in (10,31 m).

Notes: The Model 406 proposal was winning contender in the AHIP (Army Helicopter Improvement Program) competition, the first of five prototypes having flown on 6 October 1983. US Army development and operational tests were completed in March 1985, and current planning calls for the modification of at least 578 existing OH-58A Kiowa helicopters to OH-58D standards during 1985–91. The OH-58D features a mast-mounted sight, specialised avionics and an integrated multiplex cockpit. Armed with two air-to-air missiles, the OH-58D is intended as a close-combat reconnaissance helicopter which can support attack helicopter missions and direct artillery fire as well as perform intelligence gathering and surveillance missions.

BELL MODEL 412

Country of Origin: USA.
Type: Fifteen-seat utility transport helicopter.
Power Plant: One 1,800 shp Pratt & Whitney PT6T-3B-1 turboshaft.
Performance: Max speed, 149 mph (240 km/h) at sea level; cruise, 143 mph (230 km/h) at sea level, 146 mph (235 km/h) at 5,000 ft (1 525 m); hovering ceiling (in ground effect), 10,800 ft (3 290 m), (out of ground effect), 7,100 ft (2 165 m) at 10,500 lb/4 763 kg; max range, 282 mls (454 km), (with auxiliary tanks), 518 mls (834 km).
Weights: Empty equipped, 6,535 lb (2 964 kg); max take-off, 11,900 lb (5 397 kg).
Dimensions: Rotor diam, 46 ft 0 in (14,02 m); fuselage length, 41 ft 8½ in (12,70 m).
Notes: The Model 412, flown for the first time in August 1979, is an updated Model 212 (production of which was continuing at the beginning of 1986) with a new-design four-bladed rotor, a shorter rotor mast assembly, and uprated engine and transmission systems, giving more than twice the life of the Model 212 units. Composite rotor blades are used and the rotor head incorporates elastomeric bearings and dampers to simplify moving parts. An initial series of 200 helicopters was laid down with customer deliveries commencing February 1981. Licence manufacture is undertaken by Agusta in Italy, a military version being designated AB 412 Griffon, and is also to be undertaken by Nurtanio in Indonesia.

BOEING VERTOL 414 CHINOOK

Country of Origin: USA.

Type: Medium transport helicopter.

Power Plant: Two 3,750 shp Avco Lycoming T55-L-712 turboshafts.

Performance: (At 45,400 lb/20 593 kg) Max speed, 146 mph (235 km/h) at sea level; average cruise, 131 mph (211 km/h); max inclined climb, 1,380 ft/min (7,0 m/sec); service ceiling, 8,400 ft (2 560 m); max ferry range, 1,190 mls (1 915 km).

Weights: Empty, 22,591 lb (10 247 kg); max take-off, 50,000 lb (22 680 kg).

Dimensions: Rotor diam (each), 60 ft 0 in (18,29 m); fuselage length, 51 ft 0 in (15,55 m).

Notes: The Model 414 as supplied to the RAF as the Chinook HC Mk 1 combines some features of the US Army's CH-47D (see 1980 edition) and features of the Canadian CH-147, but with provision for glassfibre/carbonfibre rotor blades. The first of 33 Chinook HC Mk 1s for the RAF was flown on 23 March 1980 and accepted on 2 December 1980, with deliveries continuing through 1981, three more being ordered in 1982 and five in 1983. The RAF version can accommodate 44 troops and has three external cargo hooks. During 1981, Boeing Vertol initiated the conversion to essentially similar CH-47D standards a total of 436 CH-47As, Bs and Cs, and this programme is continuing throughout 1986. Eighteen Model 414s have been purchased by the Spanish Army.

EH INDUSTRIES EH 101

Countries of Origin: United Kingdom and Italy.
Type: Shipboard ant-submarine warfare helicopter and commercial transport and utility helicopter.
Power Plant: Three 1,730 shp General Electric T700-401 (CT7-6A) turboshafts.
Performance: (Estimated) Max cruising speed, 176 mph (283 km/h) at sea level; tactical radius (with 19 troops), 230 mls (370 km); range (commercial transport version with 30 passengers), 633 mls (1 020 km); ferry range, 1,150 mls (1 850 km); endurance (naval version on station with full mission load), 5 hrs.
Weights: Basic empty, 15,500 lb (7 031 kg); max take-off (naval version), 28,660 lb (13 000 kg), (commercial transport), 31,500 lb (14 290 kg).
Dimensions: Rotor diam, 61 ft 0 in (18,59 m); overall length (rotors turning), 75 ft 1½ in (22,90 m).
Notes: EH Industries comprises Westland Helicopters of the UK and Agusta of Italy, the company having been formed specifically for the development of the multi-role EH 101. The first of nine development EH 101s is scheduled to commence flight test late in 1986, the remaining eight being expected to join the test programme within a period of two years. First deliveries of the commercial version are planned to commence in 1989, with deliveries of the naval version starting in the following year. Final assembly lines are to be established in both the UK and in Italy.

HILLER RH-1100M HORNET

Country of Origin: USA.

Type: Light two/five-seat combat helicopter.

Power Plant: One 274 shp Allison 250-C20B turboshaft.

Performance: Max speed, 127 mph (204 km/h) at sea level; econ cruise, 102 mph (164 km/h); max inclined climb, 1,550 ft/min (7,87 m/sec); hovering ceiling (in ground effect), 17,000 ft (5 180 m), (out of ground effect), 11,975 ft (3 650 m); range, 396 mls (637 km) at 5,000 ft (1 525 m), (with auxiliary fuel), 615 mls (990 km).

Weights: Empty (scout), 1,600 lb (726 kg), (TOW) 2,310 lb (1 048 kg); mission, 3,100 lb (1 406 kg).

Dimensions: Rotor diam, 35 ft 5 in (10,80 m); fuselage length, 29 ft 11½ in (9,13 m).

Notes: The RH-1100M is a light attack and scout derivative of the commercial RH-1100 five seat utility helicopter and was flown for the first time in April 1985. It features an M-65 telescope (TOW) sight offset to port in the nose, and NATO-standard quick-change pylons on outriggers which can carry four tube-launched, optically-tracked, wire-guided (TOW) missiles, or a mix of 40-mm grenade launchers, 7,62-mm or 12,7-mm gun pods, or 2·75-in folding-fin rocket pods. The RH-1100M is indirectly derived, via the FH-1100 and FH-1100C commercial utility helicopters, from Hiller's unsuccessful OH-5A contender for the US Army's LOH competition. It is claimed to be the lowest cost light multi-mission and attack helicopter currently on the market.

232

KAMOV KA-27 (HELIX)

Country of Origin: USSR.
Type: (Ka-27) Shipboard anti-submaribne warfare and (Ka-32) utility transport helicopter.
Power Plant: Two 2,205 shp Isotov TV3-117V turboshafts.
Performance: (Ka-32) Max speed, 155 mph (250 km/h); max continuous cruise, 143 mph (230 km/h); max range, 497 mls (800 km); service ceiling (at 24,250 lb/11 000 kg), 16,405 ft (5 000 m).
Weights: (Ka-32) Normal loaded, 24,250 lb (11 000 kg); max loaded (with external load), 27,778 lb (12 600 kg).
Dimensions: Rotor diam (each), 52 ft 1⅞ in (15,90 m); overall length, 37 ft 0⅞ in (11,30 m).
Notes: Believed to have flown in prototype form in 1979–80, and first seen in ASW Ka-27 form during Zapad-81 exercises in the Baltic in September 1981, this Kamov helicopter has also been developed for civil roles as the Ka-32, variants including a dedicated search-and-rescue variant, the Ka-32S. The naval Ka-27 and civil Ka-32 appear to differ in no fundamental respect apart from equipment, and the former is now the standard aboard carriers of the Soviet Navy in basic ASW Helix-A form and in Helix-B form for missile target acquisition and mid-course guidance. The Ka-32S is capable of adverse weather and day or night operation, and is equipped with a 661-lb (300-kg) capacity winch for the ASR role. A slung load of up to five *tonnes* (11,023 lb) can be lifted by this version.

MBB BO 105LS

Country of Origin: Federal Germany.
Type: Five/six-seat light utility helicopter.
Power Plant: Two 550 shp Allison 250-C28C turboshafts.
Performance: Max speed, 168 mph (270 km/h) at sea level; max cruise, 157 mph (252 km/h) at sea level; max climb, 1,970 ft/min (10 m/sec); hovering ceiling (in ground effect), 13,120 ft (4 000 m), (out of ground effect), 11,280 ft (3 440 m); range, 286 mls (460 km).
Weights: Empty, 2,756 lb (1 250 kg); max take-off, 5,291 lb (2 400 kg), (with external load), 5,512 lb (2 500 kg).
Dimensions: Rotor diam, 32 ft 3½ in (9,84 m); fuselage length, 28 ft 1 in (8,56 m).
Notes: The BO 105LS is a derivative of the BO 105CB (see 1979 edition) with uprated transmission and more powerful turboshaft for "hot-and-high" conditions. It is otherwise similar to the BO 105CBS Twin Jet II (420 shp Allison 250-C20B) which was continuing in production at the beginning of 1986, when some 1,100 BO 105s (all versions) had been delivered and production was running at five monthly, and licence assembly has been undertaken in Indonesia, the Philippines and Spain. Deliveries to the Federal German Army of 227 BO 105M helicopters for liaison and observation tasks commenced late 1979, and deliveries of 212 HOT-equipped BO 105Ps for the anti-armour role began on 4 December 1980 and were completed mid-1984. The latter have uprated engines and transmission systems.

MBB-KAWASAKI BK 117

Countries of Origin: Federal Germany and Japan.
Type: Multi-purpose eight-to-twelve-seat helicopter.
Power Plant: Two 600shp Avco Lycoming LTS 101-650B-1 turboshafts.
Performance: Max speed, 171 mph (275 km/h) at sea level; cruise, 164 mph (264 km/h) at sea level; max climb, 1,970 ft/min (10 m/sec); hovering ceiling (in ground effect), 13,450 ft (4 100 m), (out of ground effect), 10,340 ft (3 150 m); range (max payload), 339 mls (545,4 km).
Weights: Empty, 3,351 lb (1 520 kg); max take-off, 6,173 lb (2 800 kg).
Dimensions: Rotor diam, 36 ft 1 in (11,00 m); fuselage length, 32 ft 5 in (9,88 m).
Notes: The BK 117 is a co-operative development between Messerschmitt-Bölkow-Blohm and Kawasaki, the first of two flying prototypes commencing its flight test programme on 13 June 1979 (in Germany), with the second following on 10 August (in Japan). A decision to proceed with series production was taken in 1980, with first flying on 24 December 1981, and production deliveries commencing first quarter of 1983 in which year 20 were delivered. A further 20 were built in 1984, and production tempo was two monthly at the beginning of 1986. MBB is responsible for the main and tail rotor systems, tail unit and hydraulic components, while Kawasaki is responsible for production of the fuselage, undercarriage and transmission.

McDONNELL DOUGLAS 500MD DEFENDER II

Country of Origin: USA.
Type: Light gunship and multi-role helicopter.
Power Plant: One 420 shp Allison 250-C20B turboshaft.
Performance: (At 3,000 lb/1 362 kg) Max speed, 175 mph (282 km/h) at sea level; cruise, 160 mph (257 km/h) at 4,000 ft (1 220 m); max inclined climb, 1,920 ft/min (9,75 m/sec); hovering ceiling (in ground effect), 8,800 ft (2 682 m), (out of ground effect), 7,100 ft (2 164 m); max range, 263 mls (423 km).
Weights: Empty, 1,295 lb (588 kg); max take-off (internal load), 3,000 lb (1 362 kg), (with external load), 3,620 lb (1 642 kg).
Dimensions: Rotor diam, 26 ft 5 in (8,05 m); fuselage length, 21 ft 5 in (6,52 m).
Notes: The Defender II multi-mission version of the Model 500MD was introduced mid-1980 for 1982 delivery, and features a Martin Marietta rotor mast-top sight, a General Dynamics twin-Stinger air-to-air missile pod, an underfuselage 30-mm chain gun and a pilot's night vision sensor. The Defender II can be rapidly reconfigured for anti-armour target designation, anti-helicopter, suppressive fire and transport roles. The Model 500MD TOW Defender (carrying four tube-launched optically-tracked wire-guided anti-armour missiles) is currently in service with Israel (30), South Korea (45) and Kenya (15). Production of the 500 was seven monthly at the beginning of 1986, when an upgraded version, the Model 500ME, had been introduced.

McDONNELL DOUGLAS 530F

Country of Origin: USA.
Type: Five-seat light utility helicopter.
Power Plant: One 650 shp Allison 250-C30 turboshaft.
Performance: Max cruise speed, 155 mph (250 km/h) at sea level, econ cruise, 150 mph (241 km/h) at 5,000 ft (1 525 m); max inclined climb, 1,780 ft/min (9,04 m/sec); hovering ceiling (in ground effect), 12,000 ft (3 660 m), (out of ground effect), 9,600 ft (2 925 m); range, 269 mls (434 km) at 5,000 ft (1 525 m).
Weights: Max take-off, 3,100 lb (1 406 kg).
Dimensions: Rotor diam, 27 ft 6 in (8,38 m); fuselage length, 23 ft 2½ in (7,07 m).
Notes: The Model 530F is the "hot and high" variant of the Model 500E (see 1983 edition under Hughes 500E) which is characterised by a longer, recontoured nose compared with the preceding Model 500D, offering increased leg room for front seat occupants and a 12 per cent increase in headroom for rear seat passengers. The principal difference between the Models 500E and 530F is the power plant, the former having a 520 shp 250-C20B. The Model 500E was flown on 28 January 1982, and was certificated in November 1982, and the Model 530F was flown in October 1982. Customer deliveries of the Model 530F began in January 1984, and on the following 4 May a military version, the Model 530MG, entered flight test, this being intended primarily for the light attack mission and being essentially similar to the 500ME apart from power plant.

McDONNELL DOUGLAS AH-64 APACHE

Country of Origin: USA.
Type: Tandem two-seat attack helicopter.
Power Plant: Two 1,690 shp General Electric T700-GE-701 turboshafts.
Performance: Max speed, 191 mph (307 km/h); cruise, 179 mph (288 km/h); max inclined climb, 3,200 ft/min (16,27 m/sec); hovering ceiling (in ground effect), 14,600 ft (4 453 m), (outside ground effect), 11,800 ft (3 600 m); service ceiling, 8,000 ft (2 400 m); max range, 424 mls (682 km).
Weights: Empty, 9,900 lb (4 490 kg); primary mission, 13,600 lb (6 169 kg); max take-off, 17,400 lb (7 892 kg).
Dimensions: Rotor diam, 48 ft 0 in (14,63 m); fuselage length, 48 ft 1⅞ in (14,70 m).
Notes: Winning contender in the US Army's AAH (Advanced Attack Helicopter) contest, the YAH-64 flew for the first time on 30 September 1975. Two prototypes were used for the initial trials, the first of three more with fully integrated weapons systems commenced trials on 31 October 1979, a further three following in 1980. Planned total procurement comprises 675 AH-64s through 1990, with 309 ordered by beginning of 1986, and a peak production rate of 12 monthly, deliveries having commenced during the summer of 1984. The AH-64 is armed with a single-barrel 30-mm gun based on the chain-driven bolt system and suspended beneath the forward fuselage, and eight BGM-71A TOW or 16 Hellfire laser-seeking missiles may be carried.

MIL MI-8 (HIP)

Country of Origin: USSR.
Type: Assault transport helicopter.
Power Plant: Two 1,700 shp Isotov TV2-117A turboshafts.
Performance: Max speed, 161 mph (260 km/h) at 3,280 ft (1 000 m), 155 mph (250 km/h) at sea level; max cruise, 140 mph (225 km/h); hovering ceiling (in ground effect), 6,233 ft (1 900 m), (out of ground effect), 2,625 ft (800 m); range (standard fuel), 290 mls (465 km).
Weights: (Hip-C) Empty, 14,603 lb (6 624 kg); normal loaded, 24,470 lb (11 100 kg); max take-off, 26,455 lb (12 000 kg).
Dimensions: Rotor diam, 69 ft 10¼ in (21,29 m); fuselage length, 60 ft 0¾ in (18,31 m).
Notes: Currently being manufactured at a rate of 700–800 annually, with more than 10,000 delivered for civil and military use since its debut in 1961, the Mi-8 is numerically the most important Soviet helicopter. Current military versions include the Hip-C basic assault transport, the Hip-D and -G with additional antennae and podded equipment for airborne communications, the Hip-E and the Hip-F, the former carrying up to six rocket pods and four Swatter IR-homing anti-armour missiles, and the latter carrying six Sagger wire-guided anti-armour missiles, and the Hip-J (illustrated) and -K ECM variants. The Mi-8 can accommodate 24 troops or 12 stretchers, and most have a 12,7-mm machine gun in the nose. An enhanced version, the Mi-17, is described on page 241.

MIL MI-14PL (HAZE-A)

Country of Origin: USSR.
Type: Amphibious anti-submarine helicopter.
Power Plant: Two 1,900 shp Isotov TV-3 turboshafts.
Performance: (Estimated) Max speed, 143 mph (230 km/h); max cruise, 130 mph (210 km/h); hovering ceiling (in ground effect), 5,250 ft (1 600 m), (out of ground effect), 2,295 ft (700 m); tactical radius, 124 mls (200 km).
Weights: (Estimated) Max take-off, 26,455 lb (12 000 kg).
Dimensions: Rotor diam, 69 ft 10¼ in (21,29 m); fuselage length, 59 ft 7 in (18,15 m).
Notes: The Mi-14PL amphibious anti-submarine warfare helicopter, which serves with shore-based elements of the Soviet Naval Air Force, is a derivative of the Mi-8 (see page 239) with essentially similar power plant and dynamic components to those of the later Mi-17, and much of the structure is common between the two helicopters. New features include the boat-type hull, outriggers which, housing the retractable lateral twin-wheel undercarriage members, incorporate water rudders, a search radar installation beneath the nose and a sonar "bird" beneath the tailboom root. The Haze-B is a version of the Mi-14PL used for the mine countermeasures task. The Mi-14PL possesses a weapons bay for ASW torpedoes, nuclear depth charges and other stores. This amphibious helicopter reportedly entered service in 1975 and about 140 were in Soviet Navy service by the beginning of 1986, other recipients being Bulgaria, Libya, Cuba, Poland and East Germany.

MIL MI-17 (HIP-H)

Country of Origin: USSR.

Type: Medium transport helicopter.

Power Plant: Two 1,900 shp Isotov TV3-117MT turbo-shafts.

Performance: (At 28,660 lb/13 000 kg) Max speed, 162 mph (260 km/h); max continuous cruise, 149 mph (240 km/h) at sea level; hovering ceiling (at 24,250 lb/11 000 kg out of ground effect), 5,800 ft (1 770 m); max range, 590 mls (950 km).

Weights: Empty, 15,652 lb (7 100 kg); normal loaded, 24,250 lb (11 000 kg); max take-off, 28,660 lb (13 000 kg).

Dimensions: Rotor diam, 69 ft 10$\frac{1}{4}$ in (21,29 m); fuselage length, 60 ft 5$\frac{1}{4}$ in (18,42 m).

Notes: The Mi-17 medium-lift helicopter is essentially a more powerful and modernised derivative of the late fifties technology Mi-8 (see page 239). The airframe and rotor are fundamentally unchanged, apart from some structural re-inforcement of the former, but higher-performance turboshafts afford double the normal climb rate and out-of-ground-effect hover ceiling of the earlier helicopter, and increase permissible maximum take-off weight. The Mi-17 has a crew of two–three and can accommodate 24 passengers, 12 casualty stretchers or up to 8,818 lb (4 000 kg) of freight. Externally, the Mi-17 is virtually indistinguishable from its precursor, the Mi-8, apart from marginally shorter engine nacelles and port-side tail rotor. The military version is known as Hip-H, India and Cuba being recent recipients of this version.

MIL MI-24 (HIND-D)

Country of Origin: USSR.

Type: Assault and anti-armour helicopter.

Power Plant: Two 2,200 shp Isotov TV3-117 turboshafts.

Performance: (Estimated) Max speed, 170–180 mph (273–290 km/h) at 3,280 ft (1 000 m); max cruise, 145 mph (233 km/h); max inclined climb rate, 3,000 ft/min (15,24 m/sec).

Weights: (Estimated) Normal take-off (with four missiles), 22,000 lb (10 000 kg).

Dimensions: (Estimated) Rotor diam, 55 ft 0 in (16,76 m); fuselage length, 55 ft 6 in (16,90 m).

Notes: By comparison with the Hind-A version of the Mi-24 (see 1977 edition), the Hind-D embodies a redesigned forward fuselage and is optimised for the gunship role, having tandem stations for the weapons operator (in nose) and pilot. The Hind-D can accommodate eight fully-equipped troops, has a barbette-mounted four-barrel rotary-type 12,7-mm cannon beneath the nose and can carry up to 2,800 lb (1 275 kg) of ordnance externally, including four AT-2 Swatter IR-homing anti-armour missiles and four pods each with 32 57-mm rockets. It has been exported to Afghanistan, Algeria, Bulgaria, Cuba, Czechoslovakia, East Germany, Hungary, India, Iraq, Libya, Poland and South Yemen. The Hind-E is similar but has provision for four laser-homing tube-launched Spiral anti-armour missiles, may be fitted with a twin-barrel 23-mm cannon on the starboard side of the fuselage and embodies some structural hardening, steel and titanium being substituted for aluminium in certain critical components.

MIL MI-26 (HALO)

Country of Origin: USSR.

Type: Military and commercial heavy-lift helicopter.

Power Plant: Two 11,400 shp Lotarev D-136 turboshafts.

Performance: Max speed, 183 mph (295 km/h); normal cruise, 158 mph (255 km/h); hovering ceiling (in ground effect), 14,765 ft (4 500 m), (out of ground effect), 5,905 ft (1 800 m); range (at 109,127 lb/49 500 kg), 310 mls (500 km), (at 123,457 lb/56 000 kg), 497 mls (800 km).

Weights: Empty, 62,169 lb (28 200 kg); normal loaded, 109,227 lb (49 500 kg); max take-off, 123,457 lb (56 000 kg).

Dimensions: Rotor diam, 104 ft 11⅞ in (32,00 m); fuselage length (nose to tail rotor), 110 ft 7¾ in (33,73 m).

Notes: The heaviest and most powerful helicopter ever flown, the Mi-26 first flew as a prototype on 14 December 1977, production of pre-series machines commencing in 1980, and preparations for full-scale production having begun in 1981. Featuring an innovative eight-bladed main rotor and carrying a flight crew of five, the Mi-26 has a max internal payload of 44,090 lb (20 000 kg). The freight hold is larger than that of the fixed-wing Antonov An-12 transport and at least 70 combat-equipped troops or 40 casualty stretchers can be accommodated. Although allegedly developed to a civil requirement, the primary role of the Mi-26 is obviously military and the Soviet Air Force achieved initial operational capability with the series version late 1983. During the course of 1982, the Mi-26 established new international payload-to-height records. Ten Mi-26 helicopters are to be supplied to the Indian Air Force.

SIKORSKY CH-53E SUPER STALLION

Country of Origin: USA.

Type: Amphibious assault transport helicopter.

Power Plant: Three 4,380 shp General Electric T64-GE-415 turboshafts.

Performance: (At 56,000 lb/25 400 kg) Max speed, 196 mph (315 km/h) at sea level; cruise, 173 mph (278 km/h) at sea level; max inclined climb, 2,750 ft/min (13,97 m/sec); hovering ceiling (in ground effect), 11,550 ft (3 520 m), (out of ground effect), 9,500 ft (2 895 m); range, 1,290 mls (2 075 km).

Weights: Empty, 33,226 lb (15 071 kg); max take-off, 73,500 lb (33 339 kg).

Dimensions: Rotor diam, 79 ft 0 in (24,08 m); fuselage length, 73 ft 5 in (22,38 m).

Notes: The CH-53E is a growth version of the CH-53D Sea Stallion (see 1974 edition) embodying a third engine, an uprated transmission system, a seventh main rotor blade and increased rotor diameter. The first of two prototypes was flown on 1 March 1974, and the first of two pre-production examples followed on 8 December 1975, production of two per month being divided between the US Navy and US Marine Corps at beginning of 1986, against total requirement for 160 through 1992. The CH-53E can accommodate up to 55 troops in a high-density seating arrangement. Fleet deliveries began mid-1981, and the first pre-production example of the MH-53E mine countermeasures version, 57 of which are required by the US Navy, flew September 1983.

SIKORSKY S-70C

Country of Origin: USA.
Type: Commercial transport helicopter.
Power Plant: Two 1,625 shp General Electric CT7-2C turboshafts.
Performance: Econ cruise speed, 186 mph (300 km/h); max inclined climb rate, 2,770 ft/min (14,1 m/sec); service ceiling, 17,200 ft (5,240 m); hovering ceiling (in ground effect), 8,700 ft (2 650 m), (out of ground effect), 4,800 ft (1 460 m); range (standard fuel with reserves), 294 mls (473 km) at 155 mph (250 km/h) at 3,000 ft (915 m), (max fuel without reserves), 342 mls (550 km).
Weights: Empty, 10,158 lb (4 607 kg); max take-off, 20,250 lb (9 185 kg).
Dimensions: Rotor diam, 53 ft 8 in (16,36 m); fuselage length, 50 ft 0¾ in (15,26 m).
Notes: The S-70C is a commercial derivative of the H-60 series of military helicopters, and may be configured for a variety of utility missions, such as maritime and environmental survey, mineral exploration and external lift, provision being made for an 8,000-lb (3 629-kg) capacity external cargo hook. Options include a winterisation kit, a cabin-mounted rescue hoist and an aeromedical evacuation kit. The S-70C has a flight deck crew of two and can accommodate 12 passengers in standard cabin configuration or up to 19 passengers in high density layout. Twenty-four were being delivered to China during 1985, but no other customers for this version had been announced.

SIKORSKY S-70 (UH-60A) BLACK HAWK

Country of Origin: USA.

Type: Tactical transport helicopter.

Power Plant: Two 1,543 shp General Electric T700-GE-700 turboshafts.

Performance: Max speed, 224 mph (360 km/h) at sea level; cruise, 166 mph (267 km/h); vertical climb rate, 450 ft/min (2,28 m/sec); hovering ceiling (in ground effect), 10,000 ft (3 048 m), (out of ground effect), 5,800 ft (1 758 m); endurance, 2·3-3·0 hrs.

Weights: Design gross, 16,500 lb (7 485 kg); max take-off, 22,000 lb (9 979 kg).

Dimensions: Rotor diam, 53 ft 8 in (16,23 m); fuselage length, 50 ft 0¾ in (15,26 m).

Notes: The Black Hawk was winner of the US Army's UTTAS (Utility Tactical Transport Aircraft System) contest. The first of three YUH-60As was flown on 17 October 1974, and a company-funded fourth prototype flew on 23 May 1975. The Black Hawk is primarily a combat assault squad carrier, accommodating 11 fully-equipped troops. Variants under development at the beginning of 1985 were the EH-60A ECM model and the HH-60A Night Hawk rescue helicopter (see page 246). The USAF is expected to procure 90 HH-60s and 77 EH-60s. The first production deliveries of the UH-60A to the US Army were made in June 1979, with some 750 delivered by beginning of 1986 against requirement for 1,107. S-70A export version has been offered to the Israeli Air Force and other air arms.

SIKORSKY S-70 (HH-60A) NIGHT HAWK

Country of Origin: USA.

Type: All-weather combat rescue helicopter.

Power Plant: Two 1,543 shp General Electric T700-GE-700 turboshafts.

Performance: Max speed, 167 mph (268 km/h) at sea level; max cruise, 147 mph (238 km/h) at 4,000 ft (1 220 m); hovering ceiling (in ground effect), 9,500 ft (2 895 m), (out of ground effect), 5,600 ft (1 705 m); endurance (max fuel), 4 hr 51 min.

Weights: Empty, 12,642 lb (5 734 kg); max take-off (mission), 20,413 lb (9 259 kg), (alternative), 22,000 lb (9 979 kg).

Dimensions: Rotor diam, 53 ft 8 in (16,36 m); fuselage length (excluding refuelling probe), 50 ft 0¾ in (15,26 m).

Notes: The HH-60A Night Hawk is an optimised USAF rescue version of the US Army's UH-60A Black Hawk intended to undertake unescorted day/night missions at treetop level over a radius of 287 miles (463 km) from a friendly base without flight refuelling. The prototype was flown on 4 February 1984, and the USAF plans to procure 90 Night Hawks with deliveries commencing in 1988, the series model having T700-GE-401 turboshafts rated at 1,690 shp. Accommodation is provided for a crew of two and 10 passengers, or four litters and three seated casualties/medical attendants. Defensive equipment to be installed in the HH-60A will include 7,62-mm machine guns, a radar warning receiver, a flare/chaff dispenser and an infra-red jammer.

SIKORSKY S-70L (SH-60B) SEA HAWK

Country of Origin: USA.
Type: Shipboard multi-role helicopter.
Power Plant: Two 1,690 shp General Electric T700-GE-401 turboshafts.
Performance: (At 20,244 lb/9 183 kg) Max speed, 167 mph (269 km/h) at sea level; max cruising speed, 155 mph (249 km/h) at 5,000 ft (1 525 m); max vertical climb, 1,192 ft/min (6,05 m/sec); time on station (at radius of 57 mls/92 km), 3 hrs 52 min.
Weights: Empty equipped, 13,678 lb (6 204 kg); max take-off, 21,844 lb (9 908 kg).
Dimensions: Rotor diam, 53 ft 8 in (16,36 m); fuselage length, 50 ft 0¾ in (15,26 m).
Notes: Winner of the US Navy's LAMPS (Light Airborne Multi-Purpose System) Mk III helicopter contest, the SH-60B is intended to fulfil both anti-submarine warfare (ASW) and anti-ship surveillance and targeting (ASST) missions, and the first of five prototypes was flown on 12 December 1979, and the last on 14 July 1980. Evolved from the UH-60A (see page 246), the SH-60B is intended to serve aboard DD-963 destroyers, DDG-47 Aegis cruisers and FFG-7 guided-missile frigates as an integral extension of the sensor and weapon system of the launching vessel. The US Navy has a requirement for 204 SH-60Bs, the first of which was delivered in October 1983, and for 175 simplified SH-60Fs without MAD gear.

SIKORSKY S-76B

Country of Origin: USA.

Type: Commercial transport helicopter.

Power Plant: Two 960 shp Pratt & Whitney (Canada) PT6B-36 turboshafts.

Performance: (Manufacturer's estimates) Max cruise speed, 167 mph (269 km/h); econ cruise, 155 mph (250 km/h); max inclined climb, 1,700 ft/min (8,63 m/sec); service ceiling, 16,000 ft (4 875 m); hovering ceiling (in ground effect), 8,700 ft (2 650 m), (out of ground effect), 5,900 ft (1 800 m); range (max payload), 207 mls (333 km), (max standard fuel), 414 mls (667 km).

Weights: Empty, 6,250 lb (2 835 kg); max take-off, 11,000 lb (4 989 kg).

Dimensions: Rotor diam, 44 ft 0 in (13,41 m); fuselage length, 43 ft 4½ in (13,22 m).

Notes: The S-76B is a derivative of the S-76 Mk II (see 1984 edition) from which it differs primarily in the type of power plant. A prototype of the S-76B was flown for the first time on 22 June 1984, and first customer deliveries were effected the first half of 1985. Offering a 51 per cent increase in useful load under hot and high conditions by comparison with the S-76 Mk II, the S-76B provides accommodation for a flight crew of two and a maximum of 12 passengers. A total of some 300 S-76 helicopters (all versions) had been delivered by the beginning of 1986. Commercial and military (AUH-76) utility versions are available.

WESTLAND SEA KING

Country of Origin: United Kingdom (US licence).

Type: Anti-submarine warfare and search-and-rescue helicopter.

Power Plant: Two 1,660 shp Rolls-Royce Gnome H.1400-1 turboshafts.

Performance: Max speed, 143 mph (230 km/h); max continuous cruise at sea level, 131 mph (211 km/h); hovering ceiling (in ground effect), 5,000 ft (1 525 m), (out of ground effect), 3,200 ft (975 m); range (standard fuel), 764 mls (1 230 km), (auxiliary fuel), 937 mls (1 507 km).

Weights: Empty equipped (ASW), 13,672 lb (6 201 kg), (SAR), 12,376 lb (5 613 kg); max take-off, 21,000 lb (9 525 kg).

Dimensions: Rotor diam, 62 ft 0 in (18,90 m); fuselage length, 55 ft 9¾ in (17,01 m).

Notes: The Sea King Mk 2 is an uprated version of the basic ASW and SAR derivative of the licence-built S-61D (see 1982 edition), the first Mk 2 being flown on 30 June 1974, and being one of 10 Sea King Mk 50s ordered by the Australian Navy. Twenty-one to the Royal Navy as HAS Mk 2s, and 19 examples of a SAR version to the RAF as HAR Mk 3s. Current production version is the HAS Mk 5, delivery of 17 to Royal Navy having commenced October 1980, and a further 13 subsequently being ordered. All HAS Mk 2s being brought up to Mk 5 standards and eight Mks 2 and 3 fitted with Thorn-EMI searchwater radar for airborne early warning duty.

WESTLAND LYNX 3

Country of Origin: United Kingdom.
Type: Two-seat anti-armour helicopter.
Power Plant: Two 1,115 shp Rolls-Royce Gem 60 turbo-shafts.
Performance: (Manufacturer's estimates) Max speed, 190 mph (306 km/h) at sea level; cruise, 172 mph (278 km/h); range (max fuel and 20 min reserves), 385 mls (620 km); endurance, 3·5 hrs.
Weights: Normal max take-off, 13,000 lb (5 896 kg).
Dimensions: Rotor diam, 42 ft 0 in (12,80 m); length (main rotor folded), 45 ft 3 in (13,79 m).
Notes: Derived from the earlier production Lynx (see 1984 edition), the Lynx 3 is a dedicated anti-armour helicopter, a prototype of which flew for the first time on 14 June 1984. Incorporating the dynamic systems of the earlier versions of the Lynx, it is engineered to afford increased survivability and can mount greater firepower. Suitable for day or night operation and in adverse weather conditions, the Lynx 3 can be armed with Stinger missiles for self defence, and can carry and launch Euromissile HOT, Hughes TOW and Rockwell Hellfire anti-armour missiles. It can also be equipped with a 20-mm cannon and a pintle-mounted 7,62-mm machine gun. The crew seats are provided with armour protection. A naval version has been proposed with 360-deg radar, MAD, dunking sonar, active and passive sonobuoys, and torpedoes, depth charges or Sea Skua missiles.

WESTLAND 30-100

Country of Origin: United Kingdom.
Type: Transport and utility helicopter.
Power Plant: Two 1,265 shp Rolls-Royce Gem 60-1 turbo-shafts.
Performance: Max speed (at 10,500 lb/4 763 kg), 163 mph (263 km/h) at 3,000 ft (915 m); hovering ceiling (in ground effect), 7,200 ft (2 195 m), (out of ground effect), 5,000 ft (1 525 m); range (seven passengers), 426 mls (686 km).
Weights: Operational empty (typical), 6,880 lb (3 120 kg); max take-off, 12,800 lb (5 806 kg).
Dimensions: Rotor diam, 43 ft 8 in (13,31 m); fuselage length, 47 ft 0 in (14,33 m).
Notes: The WG 30, flown for the first time on 10 April 1979, is a private venture development of the Lynx (see 1984 edition) featuring an entirely new fuselage offering a substantial increase in capacity. Aimed primarily at the multi-role military helicopter field, the WG 30 has a crew of two and in the transport role can carry 17–22 passengers. Commitment to the WG 30 at the time of closing for press covers initial production of 41, deliveries of which began January 1982. British Airways has purchased two and four have been supplied to the US-based Airspur Airline, other US purchasers including SFO Helicopter Airlines and Helicopter Hire. The WG 30 utilises more than 85% of the proven systems of the WG 13 Lynx, and the WG 30-200 (flown on 3 September 1983) differs from the -100 in having General Electric CT7-2 turboshafts.

INDEX OF AIRCRAFT TYPES

A 10B Wamira, Hawker de Havilland, 120
Aeritalia-Aermacchi-Embraer AMX, 6
 -Partenavia AP68TP-600 Viator, 8
Aermacchi MB-339, 10
Aérospatiale AS 332 Super Puma, 216
 AS 350 Ecureuil, 217
 AS 355 Ecureuil, 218
 SA 365 Dauphin 2, 219
 TB 30 Epsilon, 12
 -Aeritalia ATR 42, 14
Agusta A 109A Mk II, 220
 A 109K, 221
 A 129 Mangusta, 222
AH-1S HueyCobra, Bell, 223
AH-1W SuperCobra, Bell, 224
 AH-64 Apache, McDonnell Douglas, 238
AIDC AT-3 Tse Tchan, 16
Airbus A300-600, 18
 A310-300, 20
Alpha Jet, Dassault-Breguet/Dornier, 86
AMX, Aeritalia-Aermacch-Embraer, 6
Antonov An-28 (Cash), 22
 An-32 (Cline), 24
 An-72 (Coaler), 26
 An-124 Ruslan (Condor), 28
Apache, McDonnell Douglas AH-64, 238
ARV Super 2, 30
Astra, IAI Westwind, 124
Atlantic G2 (ATL2), Dassault-Breguet, 76
ATP, British Aerospace, 52
ATR 42, Aérospatiale-Aeritalia, 14
AV-8B, McDonnell Douglas, 56
Avanti, Gates-Piaggio GP-180, 108
Aviojet, CASA C-101DD, 68
Avtek 400, 32

B-1B, Rockwell, 176
Backfire-A (Tupolev), 204
Beechcraft 1900C, 34
 2000 Starship, 36
Bell 214ST, 225
 222B, 226
 400 TwinRanger, 227
 406 (OH-58D), 228
 412, 229
 AH-1S HueyCobra, 223
 AH-1W SuperCobra, 224
BK 117, Mbb-Kawasaki, 235
Black Hawk, Sikorsky UH-60A, 246
Blackjack-A (Tupolev), 204
BO 105, MBB, 234
Boeing 737-300, 38
 747-300, 40
 757-200, 42
 767-200, 44
 E-3A Sentry, 46
 Vertol 414 Chinook, 230
Brasilia, Embraer EMB-120, 92
British Aerospace 125-800, 48
 146-200, 50
 ATP, 52
 EAP, 54
 Harrier GR Mk 5, 57
 Hawk 200, 58
 Jetstream 31, 60
 Nimrod AEW Mk 3, 62
 Sea Harrier, 64

C-5B Galaxy, Lockheed, 136
C-130 Hercules, Lockheed, 138
Camber (Il-86), 130
Canadair Challenger 601, 66
Candid (Il-76), 128
Caravan I, Cessna 208, 72
Careless (Tu-154M), 206
CASA C-101DD Aviojet, 68
 -Nurtanio CH-235, 70
Cash (An-28), 22
Cessna 208 Caravan I, 72
 650 Citation III, 74
CH-53E Super Stallion, Sikorsky, 244

Chinook, Boeing Vertol 414, 230

Citation III, Cessna 650, 74

Cline (An-32), 24

Clobber (Yak-42), 214

Coaler (An-72), 26

Condor (An-124), 28

Cub (Shansi Yun-8). 182

Dash 8, de Havilland Canada, 88

Dassault-Breguet Atlantique G2, 76

  Mirage 2000, 82

  Mirage F1, 80

  Mystère-Falcon 900, 78

  Rafale, 84

  /Dornier Alpha Jet, 86

Dauphin 2, Aérospatiale SA 365, 219

Defender II, McDonnell Douglas 500MD, 236

De Havilland Canada Dash 8, 88

Dornier Do 228, 90

E-2C Hawkeye, Grumman, 112

E-3 Sentry, Boeing, 46

Eagle, McDonnell Douglas F-15C, 144

EAP, British Aerospace, 54

Ecureuil, Aérospatiale AS 350, 217

EH-101, 231

Embraer EMB-120 Brasilia, 92

  EMB-312 Tucano, 94

ENAER T-35 Pillán, 96

Epsilon, Aérospatiale TB 30, 12

Extender, McDonnell Douglas KC-10A, 148

F-14A (Plus) Tomcat, Grumman, 114

F-15C Eagle, McDonnell Douglas, 144

F-16, Fighting Falcon, General Dynamics, 110

F-20A Tigershark, Northrop, 164

F/A-18A Hornet, McDonnell Douglas, 146

Fairchild T-46A, 98

Falcon 900, Dassault-Bregeut, 78

Fantan-A (Qiang-5), 158

Fantrainer, Rhein-Flugzeugbau, 174

Fencer (Su-24), 196

Fieldmaster, Norman NDN 6, 162

Fighting Falcon, General Dynamics F-16, 110

Finback (Jian-8), 184

Fitter (Su-17), 194

Flanker (Su-27), 200

Flogger (MiG-23), 152

FMA IA 63 Pampa, 100

Fokker 50, 102

  100, 104

Forger-A (Yak-38), 212

Foxhound (Mig-31), 156

Freelance, Norman NAC 1, 160

Frogfoot (Su-25), 198

Fulcrum (MiG-29), 154

Galaxy, Lockheed C-5B, 136

Galeb 4, SOKO, 192

Gates Learjet 55, 106

  -Piaggio GP-180 Avanti, 108

General Dynamics F-16 Fighting Falcon, 110

Grumman E-2C Hawkeye, 112

  F-14A (Plus) Tomcat, 114

Gulfstream Aerospace Gulfstream IV, 116

Halo (Mi-28), 243

Harbin Yun-12 Turbo-Panda, 118

Harrier GR Mk 5, British Aerospace, 56

Hawk 200, British Aerospace, 58

Hawker de Havilland A 10 Wamira, 120

Hawkeye, Grumman E-2C, 112

Haze-A (Mi-14PL), 240

Helix (Ka-27), 233
Hercules, Lockheed L-100-30, 138
HH-60H Night Hawk, Sikorsky, 247
Hiller RH-1100M Hornet, 232
Hind (Mi-24), 242
Hip (Mi-8), 239
Hornet, Hiller RH-1100M, 232
Hornet, McDonnell Douglas F/A-18A, 146
HueyCobra, Bell AH-1S, 223

IAI Lavi, 122
   Westwind Astra, 124
IAv Craiova IAR-99 Soim, 126
Ilyushin Il-76 (Candid), 128
   Il-86 (Camber), 130

Jetstream 31, British Aerospace, 60
Jian-8 (Finback), Shenyang, 184

Kamov Ka-27 (Helix), 233
   Ka-32 (Helix), 233
Kawasaki T-4, 132
KC-10A Extender, McDonnell Douglas, 148

Lasta, UTVA, 208
Lavi, IAI, 122
Learjet 55, Gates, 106
LET L-41OUVP-E Turbolet, 134
Lockheed C-5B Galaxy, 136
   L-100-30 Hercules, 138
   P-3C Orion, 140
   (MCE) TriStar K Mk 1, 142
Lynx 3, Westland, 251

Mainstay (Ilyushin), 128
Malibu, Piper PA-46-310P, 170
Mangusta, Agusta A 129, 222
MB-339, Aermacchi, 10
MBB BO 105, 234
   -Kawasaki BK 117, 235
McDonnell Douglas 500MD Defender II, 236
   530F, 237

AH-64 Apache, 238
AV-8B, 56
F-15C Eagle, 144
F/A-18A Hornet, 146
KC-10A Extender, 148
MD-80, 150
Mikoyan MiG-23 (Flogger), 152
   MiG-29 (Fulcrum), 154
   MiG-31 (Foxhound), 156
Mil Mi-8 (Hip), 239
   Mi-14PL (Haze), 240
   Mi-17 (Hip), 241
   Mi-24 (Hind-D), 242
   Mi-28 (Halo), 243
Mirage 2000, Dassault-Breguet, 82
   F1, Dassault-Breguet, 80
Mystère 900, Dassault-Breguet, 78

Nanchang Qiang-5 (Fantan-A), 158
Night Hawk, Sikorsky HH-60A, 247
Nimrod AEW Mk 3, British Aerospace, 62
Norman NAC 1 Freelance, 160
   NDN 6 Fieldmaster, 162
Northrop F-20A Tigershark, 164

OH-58D, Bell, 228
Orao 2, SOKO, 190
Orion, Lockheed P-3C, 140
Orlik, PZL-130, 172

P-3C Orion, Lockheed, 140
Pampa, FMA IA 63, 100
Panavia Tornado F Mk 3, 166
Partenavia AP68TP-600 Viator, 8
Pilatus PC-9, 168
Pillán, ENAER T-35, 96
Piper PA-46-310P Malibu, 170
PZL-130 Orlik, 172

Qiang-5, Fantan-A, Nanchang, 158

Rafale, Dassault-Breguet, 84
Rhein-Flugzeugbau Fantrainer, 174
Rockwell B-1B, 176
Ruslan, Antonov An-124 (Condor), 28

Saab (JA) 37 Viggen, 178
   SF340, 180
Sea Harrier, British Aerospace, 64
Sea Hawk, Sikorsky SH-60B, 248
Sea King, Westland, 250
Sentry, Boeing E-3, 46
SH-60B Sea Hawk, Sikorsky, 248
Shansi Yun-8 (Cub), 182
Shenyang Jian-8 (Finback), 184
Shorts 360, 186
Siai Marchetti S.211, 188
Sikorsky CH-53E Super Stallion, 244
   HH-60A Night Hawk, 247
   S-70C, 245
   S-76B, 249
   SH-60B Sea Hawk, 248
   UH-60A Black Hawk, 246
Soim, IAv Craiova IAR-99, 126
SOKO Galeb 4, 192
   Orao 2, 190
Spartacus, Aeritalia-Partenavia, 8
Starship, Beechcraft 2000, 36
Sukhoi Su-17 (Fitter), 194
   Su-24 (Fencer), 196
   Su-25 (Frogfoot), 198
   Su-27 (Flanker), 200
Super 2, ARV, 30
SuperCobra, Bell AH-1W, 224
Super Galeb, SOKO, 192

Super Puma, Aérospatiale AS 332L, 216
Super Stallion, Sikorsky CH-53E, 244

T-46A, Fairchild, 98
TB 30 Epsilon, Aérospatiale, 12
Tigershark, Northrop F-20A, 164
Tomcat, Grumman F-14A (plus), 114
Tornado F Mk 3, Panavia, 166
Tucano, Embraer EMB-312, 94
Tupolev Tu-22M (Backfire-B), 202
   (Blackjack-A), 204
Turbolet, LET L-410UVP-E, 134
Turbo-Panda, Harbin Yun-12, 118
TwinRanger, Bell 400, 227

UH-60A Black Hawk, Sikorsky, 246
UTVA Lasta, 208

Valmet L-80 TP, 210
Viator, Aeritalia-Partenavia AP68TP, 8
Viggen, Saab (JA) 37, 178

Wamira, Hawker de Havilland A 10, 120
Westland 30-100, 252
   Lynx 3, 251
   Sea King, 250
Westwind Astra, IAI, 124

Yakovlev Yak-38 (Forger-A), 212
   Yak-42 (Clobber), 214
Yun-8, Shansi, 182
Yun-12 Turbo-Panda, Harbin, 118